ROOM 13

ROOM 13

ROOM 13

EDGAR WALLACE

WILDSIDE PRESS

TO MY FRIEND
Sir EMSLEY CARR, Kt.

Originally published in 1926.
Published by Wildside Press.
Visit us online at wildsidepress.com.

INTRODUCTION

KARL WURF

Edgar Wallace (1875–1932) was one of the most prolific and widely read British authors of the early 20th century. Known primarily for his crime and mystery novels, Wallace built an extraordinary reputation during his lifetime, producing more than 170 books, countless short stories, plays, and journalism. His work was once so popular that it was said one out of every four books read in England in the 1920s bore his name. Despite his vast output, his stories consistently combined suspense, pace, and a keen eye for the darker corners of human ambition.

Wallace's early life shaped his outlook and literary energy. Born into poverty in London, he left school at twelve and worked a variety of odd jobs before joining the army. His military service in South Africa during the Boer War exposed him to both colonial politics and human conflict, subjects that often found their way into his adventure fiction. He later worked as a war correspondent, experiences that sharpened his journalistic instincts and his gift for swift, gripping narrative.

In terms of influences, Wallace owed much to Victorian and Edwardian popular literature. The adventure tales of H. Rider Haggard and the detective stories of Arthur Conan Doyle provided him with models for blending action with mystery. He also absorbed the brisk narrative style of contemporary journalists, giving his fiction a pace that appealed to readers of newspapers as much as to traditional novel audiences. At the same time, Wallace's emphasis on criminal underworlds, daring heists, and complex conspiracies anticipated the hardboiled fiction that would flourish later in America.

Wallace's place in literature is sometimes overlooked because of his sheer productivity, which caused critics to treat him as a craftsman rather than an artist. Yet his role in shaping modern popular fiction is undeniable. He helped define the modern thriller, laying groundwork for writers such as James Hadley Chase and Ian Fleming. His novel *King Kong*, adapted into the famous 1933 film, ensured him a permanent place in cultural history.

Room 13 is part of the popular J.G. Reeder series, featuring one of Wallace's most distinctive creations. Reeder, a mild-looking civil servant with an unassuming manner, conceals a brilliant and unorthodox mind for criminal detection. Unlike the flamboyant detectives of the time, Reeder relies on patience, observation, and psychological insight, making him a refreshing contrast in the genre. The stories often balance elements of mystery with the tension of crime thrillers, and *Room 13* stands out for its tightly plotted drama and the cleverness of its central figure. The Reeder books proved especially influential in shaping portrayals of the "ordinary" detective whose quiet methods mask extraordinary results.

Readers drawn to Wallace often admire his ability to balance suspense and atmosphere with direct, clear storytelling. His prose may lack the polish of more "literary" contemporaries, but his gift for plot construction and his instinct for dramatic tension remain remarkable. For those who enjoy tightly wound mysteries, labyrinthine plots, and a steady drumbeat of danger, Wallace's novels still deliver the thrills they promised nearly a century ago.

Among his works most worth exploring are *The Four Just Men*, a daring tale of vigilante justice; *The Green Archer*, a gothic-flavored mystery mixing medieval legend with modern crime; *Sanders of the River*, which reflects his colonial experiences in Africa; and *The Crimson Circle*, a fast-paced story of blackmail and murder. These books, along with dozens of others, showcase the range of Edgar Wallace's storytelling and secure his legacy as one of the key architects of modern crime and adventure fiction.

CHAPTER 1

Over the grim stone archway was carved the words:

PARCERE SUBJECTIS.

In cold weather, and employing the argot of his companions, Johnny Gray translated this as "Parky Subjects"—it certainly had no significance as "Spare the Vanquished," for he had been neither vanquished nor spared.

Day by day, harnessed to the shafts, he and Lal Morgon had pulled a heavy hand-cart up the steep slope, and day by day had watched absently the red-bearded gate-warder put his key in the big polished lock and snap open the gates. And then the little party had passed through, an armed warder leading, an armed warder behind, and the gate had closed.

And at four o'clock he had walked back under the archway and halted whilst the gate was unlocked and the hand-cart admitted.

Every building was hideously familiar. The gaunt "halls," pitch painted against the Dartmoor storms, the low-roofed office, the gas house, the big, barn-like laundry, the ancient bakery, the exercise yard with its broken asphalt, the ugly church, garishly decorated, the long, scrubbed benches with the raised seats for the warders… and the graveyard where the happily released lifers rested from their labours.

One morning in spring, he went out of the gate with a working party. They were building a shed, and he had taken the style and responsibility of bricklayer's labourer. He liked the work because you can talk more freely on a job like that, and he wanted to hear all that Lal Morgon had to say about the Big Printer.

"Not so much talking today," said the warder in charge, seating himself on a sack-covered brick heap.

"No, sir," said Lal.

He was a wizened man of fifty and a lifer, and he had one ambition, which was to live long enough to get another "lagging."

"But not burglary, Gray," he said as he leisurely set a brick in its place; "and not shootin', like old Legge got his packet. And not faking Spider King, like you got yours."

"I didn't get mine for faking Spider King," said Johnny calmly. "I didn't know that Spider King had been rung in when I took him on the course, and was another horse altogether. They framed up Spider King to catch me. I am not complaining."

"I know you're innocent—everybody is," said Lal soothingly. "I'm the only guilty man in boob. That's what the governor says. 'Morgon,' he says, 'it does my heart good to meet a guilty man that ain't the victim of circumstantiality. Like everybody else is in boob,' he says."

Johnny did not pursue the subject. There was no reason why he should. This fact was beyond dispute. He had known all about the big race-course swindles that were being worked, and had been an associate of men who backed the "rung in" horses. He accepted the sentence of three years' penal servitude that had been passed without appeal or complaint. Not because he was guilty of the act for which he was charged—there was another excellent reason.

"If they lumbered you with the crime, it was because you was a mug," said old Lal complacently. "That's what mugs are for—to be lumbered. What did old Kane say?"

"I didn't see Mr. Kane," said Johnny shortly.

"He'd think you was a mug, too," said Lal with satisfaction—"hand me a brick, Gray, and shut up! That nosey screw's coming over."

The "nosey screw" was no more inquisitive than any other warder. He strolled across, the handle of his truncheon showing from his pocket, the well-worn strap dangling.

"Not so much talking," he said mechanically.

"I was asking for a brick, sir," said Lal humbly. "These bricks ain't so good as the last lot."

"I've noticed that," said the warder, examining a half-brick with a professional and disapproving eye.

"Trust you to notice that, sir," said the sycophant with the right blend of admiration and awe. And, when the warder had passed:

"That boss-eyed perisher don't know a brick from a gas-stove," said Lal without heat. "He's the bloke that old Legge got straightened when he was in here—used to have private letters brought in every other day. But then, old Legge's got money. Him and Peter Kane smashed the strong-room of the *Orsonic* and got away with a million dollars. They never caught Peter, but Legge was easy. He shot a copper and got life."

Johnny had heard Legge's biography a hundred times, but Lal Morgon had reached the stage of life when every story he told was new.

"That's why he hates Peter," said the garrulous bricklayer. "That's why young Legge and him are going to get Peter. And young Legge's hot! Thirty years of age by all accounts, and the biggest printer of slush in the world! And it's not ord'nary slush. Experts get all mixed up when they see young Legge's notes—can't tell 'em from real Bank of England stuff. And the police *and* the secret service after him for years—and then never got him!"

The day was warm, and Lal stripped off his red and blue striped working jacket. He wore, as did the rest of the party, the stained yellow breeches faintly stamped with the broad arrow. Around his calves were buttoned yellow gaiters. His shirt was of stout cotton, white with narrow blue stripes, and on his head was a cap adorned with mystic letters of the alphabet to indicate the dates of his convictions. A week later, when the letters were abolished, Lal Morgon had a grievance. He felt as a soldier might feel when he was deprived of his decorations.

"You've never met young Jeff?" stated rather than asked Lal, smoothing a dab of mortar with a leisurely touch.

"I've seen him—I have not met him," said Johnny grimly, and something in his tone made the old convict look up.

"He 'shopped' me," said Johnny, and Lal indicated his surprise with an inclination of his head that was ridiculously like a bow.

"I don't know why, but I do know that he 'shopped' me," said Johnny. "He was the man who fixed up the fake, got me persuaded to bring the horse on to the course, and then squeaked. Until then I did not know that the alleged Spider King was in reality Boy Saunders cleverly camouflaged."

"Squeaking's hidjus," said the shocked Lal, and he seemed troubled. "And Emanuel Legge's boy, too! Why did he do it—did you catch him over money?"

Johnny shook his head.

"I don't know. If it's true that he hates Peter Kane he may have done it out of revenge, knowing that I'm fond of Peter, and... well, I'm fond of Peter. He warned me about mixing with the crowd I ran with—"

"*Stop that talking, will you!*"

They worked for some time in silence. Then:

"That screw will get somebody hung one of these days," said Lal in a tone of quiet despair. "He's the feller that little Lew Morse got a bashing for—over clouting him with a spanner in the blacksmith's shop. He was nearly killed. What a pity! Lew wasn't much account, an' he's often said he'd as soon be dead as sober."

At four o'clock the working party fell in and marched or shuffled down the narrow road to the prison gates.

Parcere Subjectis.

Johnny looked up and winked at the grim jest, and he had the illusion that the archway winked back at him. At half-past four, he turned into the deep-recessed doorway of his cell, and the yellow door closed on him with a metallic snap of a lock.

It was a big, vaulted cell, and the colour of the folded blanket ends gave it a rakish touch of gaiety. On a shelf in one corner was a photograph of a fox terrier, a pretty head turned inquiringly toward him.

He poured out a mugful of water and drank it, looking up at the barred window. Presently his tea would come, and then the lock would be put on for eighteen and a half hours. And for eighteen and a half hours he must amuse himself as best he could. He could read whilst the light held—a volume of travel was on the ledge that served as a table. Or he could write on his slate, or draw horses and dogs, or work out interminable problems in mathematics, or write poetry... or think.

That was the worst exercise of all. He crossed the cell and took down the photograph. The mount had worn limp with much handling, and he looked with a half-smile into the big eyes of the terrier.

"It is a pity you can't write, old Spot," he said.

Other people could write, and did, he thought as he replaced the photograph. But Peter Kane never once mentioned Marney, and Marney had not written since... a long time. It was ominous, informative, in some ways decisive. A brief reference, "Marney is well," or "Marney thanks you for your inquiry," and that was all.

The whole story was clearly written in those curt phrases, the story of Peter's love of the girl, and his determination that she should not marry a man with the prison taint. Peter's adoration of his daughter was almost a mania—her happiness and her future came first, and must always be first. Peter loved him—Johnny had sensed that. He had given him the affection that a man might give his grown son. If this tragic folly of his had not led to the entanglement which brought him to a convict prison, Peter would have given Marney to him, as she was willing to give herself.

"That's that," said Johnny in his rôle of philosopher.

And then came tea and the final lock up, and silence... and thoughts again.

Why did young Legge trap him? He had only seen the man once; they had never even met. It was only by chance that he had ever seen this young printer of forged notes. He could not guess that he was known to the man he "shopped," for Jeff Legge was an illusive person. One never met him in the usual rendezvous where the half-underworld foregather to boast and plot or drink and love.

A key rattled in the lock, and Johnny got up. He forgot that it was the evening when the chaplain visited him.

"Sit down, Gray." The door closed on the clergyman, and he seated himself on Johnny's bed.

It was curious that he should take up the thread of Johnny's interrupted thoughts.

"I want to get your mind straight about this man Legge... the son, I mean. It is pretty bad to brood on grievances, real or fancied, and you are nearing the end of your term of imprisonment, when your resentment will have a chance of expressing itself. And, Gray, I don't want to see you here again."

Johnny Gray smiled.

"You won't see me *here*!" he emphasised the word. "As to Jeff Legge, I know little about him, though I've done some fairly fluent guessing and I've heard a lot."

The chaplain shook his head thoughtfully.

"I have heard a little; he's the man they call the Big Printer, isn't he? Of course, I know all about the flooding of Europe with spurious notes, and that the police had failed to catch the man who was putting them into circulation. Is that Jeff Legge?"

Johnny did not answer, and the chaplain smiled a little sadly.

"'Thou shalt not squeak'—the eleventh commandment, isn't it?" he asked good-humouredly. "I am afraid I have been indiscreet. When does your sentence end?"

"In six months," replied Johnny, "and I'll not be sorry."

"What are you going to do? Have you any money?"

The convict's lips twitched.

"Yes, I have three thousand a year," he said quietly. "That is a fact which did not come out at the trial, for certain reasons. No, padre, money isn't my difficulty. I suppose I shall travel. I certainly shall not attempt to live down my grisly past."

"That means you're not going to change your name," said the chaplain with a twinkle in his eye. "Well, with three thousand a year, I can't see you coming here again." Suddenly he remembered. Putting his hand in his pocket, he took out a letter. "The Deputy gave me this, and I'd nearly forgotten. It arrived this morning."

The letter was opened, as were all letters that came to convicts, and Johnny glanced carelessly at the envelope. It was not, as he had expected, a letter from his lawyer. The bold handwriting was Peter Kane's—the first letter he had written for six months. He waited until the door had closed upon the visitor, and then he took the letter from the envelope. There were only a few lines of writing.

Dear Johnny,

I hope you are not going to be very much upset by the news I am telling you. Marney is marrying Major Floyd, of Toronto, and I know that you're big enough and fine enough to wish her luck. The man she is marrying is a real good fellow who will make her happy.

Johnny put down the letter on to the ledge, and for ten minutes paced the narrow length of his cell, his hands clasped behind him. Marney to be married! His face was white, tense, his eyes dark with gloom. He stopped and poured out a mugful of water with a hand that shook, then raised the glass to the barred window that looked eastward.

"Good luck to you, Marney!" he said huskily, and drank the mug empty.

CHAPTER 2

Two days later, Johnny Gray was summoned to the Governor's office and heard the momentous news

"Gray, I have good news for you. You are to be released immediately. I have just had the authority."

Johnny inclined his head.

"Thank you, sir," he said.

A warder took him to a bathroom, where he stripped, and, with a blanket about him, came out to a cubicle, where his civilian clothes were waiting. He dressed with a queer air of unfamiliarity, and went back to his cell. The warder brought him a looking-glass and a safety-razor, and he completed his toilet.

The rest of the day was his own. He was a privileged man, and could wander about the prison in his strangely-feeling attire, the envy of men whom he had come to know and to loathe; the half madmen who for a year had been whispering their futilities into his ear.

As he stood there in the hall at a loose end, the door was flung open violently, and a group of men staggered in. In the midst of them was a howling, shrieking thing that was neither man nor beast, his face bloody, his wild arms gripped by struggling warders.

He watched the tragic group as it made its way to the punishment cells.

"Fenner," said somebody under his breath. "He coshed a screw, but they can't give him another bashing."

"Isn't Fenner that twelve-year man, that's doing his full time?" asked Johnny, remembering the convict. "And he's going out tomorrow, too!"

"That's him," said his informant, one of the hall sweepers. "He'd have got out with nine, but old Legge reported him. Game to the last, eh? They can't bash him after tomorrow, and the visiting justices won't be here for a week."

Johnny remembered the case. Legge had been witness to a brutal assault on the man by one of the warders, who had since been discharged from the service. In desperation the unfortunate Fenner had hit back, and had been tried. Legge's evidence might have saved him from the flogging which followed, but Legge was too good a friend of the warders—or they were too good friends of his—to betray a "screw." So Fenner had gone to the triangle, as he would not go again.

He could not sleep the last night in the cell. His mind was on Marney. He did not reproach her for a second. Nor did he feel bitter toward her father. It was only right and proper that Peter Kane should do what was best for his girl. The old man's ever-present fear for his daughter's future was almost an obsession. Johnny guessed that when this presentable Canadian had come along, Peter had done all in his power to further the match.

Johnny Gray walked up the steep slope for the last time. A key turned in the big lock, and he stood outside the gates, a free man. The red-bearded head warder put out his hand.

"Good luck to you," he said gruffly. "Don't you come over the Alps again."

"I've given up mountain climbing," said Johnny.

He had taken his farewell of the Governor, and now the only thing to remind him of his association with the grim prison he had left was the warder who walked by his side to the station. He had some time to wait, and Johnny tried to get some information from another angle.

"No, I don't know Jeff Legge," said the warder, shaking his head. "I knew the old man: he was here until twelve months ago—you were here, too, weren't you, Gray?"

Johnny nodded.

"Mr. Jeff Legge has never been over the Alps, then?" he asked sardonically.

"No, not in this prison, and he wasn't in Parkhurst or Portland, so far as I can remember. I've been at both places. I've heard the men talking about him. They say he's clever, which means that he'll be putting out his tins one morning. Good-bye, Gray, and be good!"

Johnny gripped the outstretched hand of the man, and, when he was in the carriage, took out his silk handkerchief and wiped his hand of the last prison contact.

His servant was waiting for him at Paddington when he arrived that afternoon, and with him, straining at a leash, a small, lop-eared fox terrier, who howled his greeting long before Johnny had seen the group. In another second the dog was struggling in his arms, licking his face, his ears, his hair, and whining his joy at the reunion. There were tears in Johnny's eyes when he put the dog down on the platform.

"There are a number of letters for you, sir. Will you dine at home?"

The excellent Parker might have been welcoming his master from a short sojourn at Monte Carlo, so very unemotional was he.

"Yes, I'll dine at home," said Johnny. He stepped into the taxicab that Parker had hired, and Spot leapt after him.

"There is no baggage, sir?" asked Parker gravely through the open window.

"There is no baggage," said Johnny as gravely. "You had better ride back with me, Parker."

The man hesitated.

"It would be a very great liberty, sir," he said.

"Not so great a liberty as I have had taken with me during the past year and nine months," said Johnny.

As the cab came out into dismal Chapel Street, the greatly daring Parker asked:

"I hope you have not had too bad a time, sir?"

Johnny laughed.

"It has not been pleasant, Parker. Prisons seldom are."

"I suppose not, sir," agreed Parker, and added unnecessarily: "I have never been in prison, sir."

Johnny's flat was in Queen's Gate, and at the sight of the peaceful luxury of his study he caught his breath.

"You're a fool," he said aloud to himself.

"Yes, sir," said the obliging Parker.

That night many men came furtively to the flat in Queen's Gate, and Johnny, after admitting the first of these, called Parker into his small dining-room.

"Parker, I am told that during my absence in the country even staid men have acquired the habit of attending cinema performances?"

"Well, sir, I like the pictures myself," admitted Parker.

"Then go and find one that lasts until eleven o'clock," said Johnny.

"You mean, sir—?"

"I mean I don't want you here tonight."

Parker's face fell, but he was a good servant.

"Very good, sir," he said, and went out, wondering sorrowfully what desperate plans his master was hatching.

At half-past ten the last of the visitors took his leave.

"I'll see Peter tomorrow," said Johnny, tossing the end of his cigarette into the hall fire-place. "You know nothing of this wedding, when it is to take place?"

"No, Captain. I only know Peter slightly."

"Who is the bridegroom?"

"A swell, by all accounts—Peter is a plausible chap, and he'd pull in the right kind. A major in the Canadian Army, I've heard, and a very nice man. Peter can catch mugs easier than some people can catch flies—"

"Peter was never a mug-catcher," said John Gray sharply.

"I don't know," said the other. "There's one born every minute."

"But they take a long time to grow up, and the women get first pluck," said Johnny good-humouredly.

Parker, returning at 11.15, found his master sitting before a fire-place which was choked with burnt paper.

Johnny reached Horsham the next afternoon soon after lunch, and none who saw the athletic figure striding up the Horsham Road would guess that less than two days before he had been the inmate of a convict cell.

He had come to make his last desperate fight for happiness. How it would end, what argument to employ, he did not know. There was one, and one only, but that he could not use.

As he turned into Down Road he saw two big limousines standing one behind the other, and wondered what social event was in progress.

Manor Hill stood aloof from its suburban neighbours, a sedate, red-brick house, its walls gay with clematis. Johnny avoided the front gates and passed down a side-path which, as he knew, led to the big lawn behind, where Peter loved to sun himself at this hour.

He paused as he emerged into the open. A pretty parlourmaid was talking to an elderly man, who wore without distinction the livery of a butler. His lined face was puckered uncomfortably, and his head was bent in a listening attitude, though it was next to impossible for a man totally deaf to miss hearing all that was said.

"I don't know what sort of houses you've been in, and what sort of people you've been working for, but I can tell you that if I find you in my room again, looking in my boxes, I shall tell Mr. Kane. I won't have it, Mr. Ford!"

"No, miss," said the butler huskily.

It was not, as Johnny knew, emotion which produced the huskiness. Barney Ford had been husky from his youth—probably squawked huskily in his cradle.

"If you are a burglar and trying to keep your hand in, I understand it," the girl continued hotly, "but you're supposed to be a respectable man! I won't have this underhand prying and sneaking. Understand that! I won't have it!"

"No, miss," said the hoarse Barney.

John Gray surveyed the scene with amusement. Barney he knew very well. He had quitted the shadier walks of life when Peter Kane had found it expedient to retire from his hazardous calling. Ex-convict, ex-burglar and ex-prize-fighter, his seamy past was in some degree redeemed by his affection for the man whose bread he ate and in whose service he pretended to be, though a worse butler had never put on uniform than Barney.

The girl was pretty, with hair of dull gold and a figure that was both straight and supple. Now her face was flushed with annoyance, and the dark eyes were ablaze. Barney certainly had prying habits, the heritage of his unregenerate days. Other servants had left the house for the same reason, and Peter had cursed and threatened without wholly reforming his servitor.

The girl did not see him as she turned and flounced into the house, leaving the old man to stare after her.

"You've made her cross," said John, coming up behind him.

Barney Ford spun round and stared. Then his jaw dropped.

"Good Lord, Johnny, when did *you* come down from college?"

The visitor laughed softly.

"Term ended yesterday," he said. "How is Peter?"

Before he replied the servant blew his nose violently, all the time keeping his eye upon the new-comer.

"How long have you bin here?" he asked at length.

"I arrived at the tail-end of your conversation," said Johnny, amused. "Barney, you haven't reformed!"

Barney Ford screwed up his face into an expression of scorn.

"They think you're a hook even if you ain't one," he said. "What does she know about life? You ain't seen Peter? He's in the house; I'll tell him in a minute. *He's* all right. All beans and bacon about the girl. That fellow adores the ground she walks on. It's not natural, being fond of your kids like that. I never was." He shook his head despairingly. "There's too much lovey-dovey and not enough strap nowadays. Spare the rod and spoil the child, as the good old poet says."

John Gray turned his head at the sound of a foot upon a stone step. It was Peter, Peter radiant yet troubled. Straight as a ramrod, for all his sixty years and white hair. He was wearing a morning coat and pearl-grey waistcoat—an innovation. For a second he hesitated, the smile struck from his face, frowning, and then he came quickly his hand outstretched.

"Well, Johnny boy, had a rotten time?"

His hand fell on the young man's shoulder, his voice had the old measure of pride and affection.

"Fairly rotten," said Johnny; "but any sympathy with me is wasted. Personally, I prefer Dartmoor to Parkhurst—it is more robust, and there are fewer imbeciles."

Peter took his arm and led him to a chair beneath the big Japanese umbrella planted on the lawn. There was something in his manner, a certain awkwardness which the new-comer could not understand.

"Did you meet anybody… there… that I know, Johnny boy?"

"Legge," said the other laconically, his eyes on Peter's face.

"That's the man I'm thinking of. How is he?"

The tone was careless, but Johnny was not deceived. Peter was intensely interested.

"He's been out six months—didn't you know?"

The other's face clouded.

"Out six months? Are you sure?"

Johnny nodded.

"I didn't know."

"I should have thought you would have heard from him," said John quietly. "He doesn't love you!"

Peter's slow smile broadened.

"I know he doesn't; did you get a chance of talking with him?"

"Plenty of chances. He was in the laundry, and he straightened a couple of screws so that he could do what he liked. He hates you, Peter. He says you shopped him."

"He's a liar," said Peter calmly. "I wouldn't shop my worst enemy. He shopped himself. Johnny, the police get a reputation for smartness, but the truth, is every other criminal arrests himself. Criminals aren't clever. They wear gloves to hide their finger-prints, and then write their names in the visitors' book. Legge and I smashed the strong-room of the *Orsonic* and got away with a hundred and twenty thousand pounds in American currency—it was the last job I did. It was dead easy getting away, but Emanuel started boasting what a clever fellow he was; and he drank a bit. An honest man can drink and wake up in his own bed. But a crook who drinks says good morning to the gaoler."

He dropped the subject abruptly, and again his hand fell on the younger man's shoulder.

"Johnny, you're not feeling sore, are you?"

Johnny did not answer.

"Are you?"

And now the fight was to begin. John Gray steeled himself for the forlorn hope.

"About Marney? No, only—"

"Old boy, I had to do it." Peter's voice was urgent, pleading. "You know what she is to me. I liked you well enough to take a chance, but after they dragged you I did some hard thinking. It would have smashed me, Johnny, if she'd been your wife then. I couldn't bear to see her cry even when she was quite a little baby. Think what it would have meant to her. It was bad enough as it was. And then this fellow came along—a good, straight, clean, cheery fellow—a gentleman. And well, I'll tell you the truth—I helped him. You'll like him. He's the sort of man anybody would like. And she loves him, Johnny."

There was a silence.

"I don't bear him any ill-will. It would be absurd if I did. Only, Peter, before she marries I want to say—"

"Before she marries?" Peter Kane's voice shook. "John, didn't Barney tell you? She was married this morning."

CHAPTER 3

"Married?"

Johnny repeated the word dully.

Marney married…! It was incredible, impossible to comprehend. For a moment the stays and supports of existence dissolved into dust, and the fabric of life fell into chaos.

"Married this morning, Johnny. You'll like him. He isn't one of us, old boy. He's as straight as… well, you understand, Johnny boy? I've worked for her and planned for her all these years; I'd have been rotten if I took a chance with her future."

Peter Kane was pleading, his big hand on the other's shoulder, his fine face clouded with anxiety and the fear that he had hurt this man beyond remedy.

"I should have wired…"

"It would have made no difference," said Peter Kane almost doggedly. "Nothing could have been changed, Johnny, nothing. It had to be. If you had been convicted innocently—I don't say you weren't—I couldn't have the memory of your imprisonment hanging over her; I couldn't have endured the uncertainty myself. Johnny, I've been crook all my life—up to fifteen years ago. I take a broader view than most men because I am what I am. But she doesn't know that. Craig's here today—"

"Craig—the Scotland Yard man?"

Peter nodded, a look of faint amusement in his eyes.

"We're good friends; we have been for years. And do you know what he said this morning? He said, 'Peter, you've done well to marry that girl into the straight way,' and I know he's right."

Johnny stretched back in the deep cane chair, his hand shading his eyes, as though he found the light too strong for him.

"I'm not going to be sorry for myself," he said with a smile, and stretching out his hand, gripped Kane's arm. "You'll not have another vendetta on your hands, Peter. I have an idea that Emanuel Legge will keep you busy—"

He stopped suddenly. The ill-fitted butler had made a stealthy appearance.

"Peter," he began in his husky whisper, "he's come. Do you want to see him?"

"Who?"

"Emanuel Legge—uglier than ever."

Peter Kane's face set, mask-like.

"Where is Miss Marney—Mrs. Floyd?"

"She's gettin' into her weddin' things and falderals for the photogry-pher," said Barney. "She had 'em off once, but the photogrypher's just come, and he's puttin' up his things in the front garden. I sez to Marney—"

"You're a talkative old gentleman," said Peter grimly. "Send Emanuel through. Do you want to see him, Johnny?"

John Gray rose.

"No," he said. "I'll wander through your alleged rosary. I want nothing to remind me of The Awful Place, thank you."

Johnny had disappeared through an opening of the box hedge at the lower end of the lawn when Barney returned with the visitor.

Mr. Emanuel Legge was a man below middle height, thin of body and face, grey and a little bald. On his nose perched a pair of horn-rimmed spectacles. He stood for a second or two surveying the scene, his chin lifted, his thin lips drawn in between his teeth. His attire was shabby, a steel chain served as a watch-guard, and, as if to emphasise the rustiness of his wrinkled suit, he wore boots that were patently new and vividly yellow. Hat in hand, he waited, his eyes slowly sweeping the domain of his enemy, until at last they came to rest upon his host.

It was Peter Kane who broke the deadly silence.

"Well, Emanuel? Come over and sit down."

Legge moved slowly toward his host.

"Quite a swell place, Peter. Everything of the best, eh? Trust you! Still got old Barney, I see. Has he reformed too? That's the word, ain't it—'reformed'?"

His voice was thin and complaining. His pale blue eyes blinked coldly at the other.

"He doesn't go thieving any more, if that is what you mean," said Peter shortly, and a look of pain distorted the visitor's face.

"Don't use that word; it's low—"

"Let me take your hat." Peter held out his hand, but the man drew his away.

"No, thanks. I promised a young friend of mine that I wouldn't lose anything while I was here. How long have you been at this place, Peter?"

"About fourteen years."

Peter sat down, and the unwelcome guest followed his example, pulling his chair round so that he faced the other squarely.

"Ah!" he said thoughtfully. "Living very comfortable, plenty to eat, go out and come in when you like. Good way of spending fourteen years. Better than having the key on you four o'clock in the afternoon. Princetown's the same old place—oh, I forgot you'd never been there."

"I've motored through," said Peter coolly, deliberately, and knew that he had touched a raw place before the lips of the man curled back in a snarl.

"Oh, you've motored through!" he sneered. "I wish I'd known; I'd have hung my flags out! They ought to have decorated Princetown that day, Peter. You drove through!" he almost spat the words.

"Have a cigar?"

Emanuel Legge waved aside the invitation.

"No, thanks. I've got out of the habit—you do in fifteen years. You can get into some, too. Fifteen years is a long time out of a life."

So Emanuel had come to make trouble, and had chosen his day well. Peter took up the challenge.

"The man you shot would have been glad of a few—he died two years after," he said curtly, and all the pent fury of his sometime comrade flamed in his eyes.

"I hope he's in hell," he hissed, "the dirty flattie!" With an effort he mastered himself. "You've had a real good time, Peter? Nice house, that wasn't bought for nothing. Servants and what not *and* motoring through the moor! You're clever!"

"I admit it."

The little man's hands were trembling, his thin lips twitched convulsively.

"Leave your pal in the lurch and get away yourself, eh? Every man for himself—well, that's the law of nature, ain't it? And if you think he's going to squeak, send a line to the busies in charge of the case and drop a few hundred to 'em and there you are!" He paused, but no reply came. "That's how it's done, ain't it, Peter?"

Kane shrugged his shoulders indifferently.

"I don't know—I'm never too old to learn."

"But that's the way it's done?" insisted the man, showing his teeth again. "That's the way you keep out of boob, ain't it?"

Peter looked at his tormentor, outwardly untroubled.

"I won't argue with you," he said.

"You can't," said the other. "I'm logical." He gazed around. "This house cost a bit of money. What's half of two hundred thousand? I'm a bad counter!" Peter did not accept the opening. "It's a hundred thousand, ain't it? I got sixty thousand—you owe me forty."

"We got less than a hundred and twenty thousand pounds, if you're talking about the ship job. You got sixty thousand, which was more than your share. I paid it into your bank the day you went down."

Legge smiled sceptically.

"The newspapers said a million dollars," he murmured.

"You don't believe what you read in the newspapers, do you? Emanuel, you're getting childish." Then suddenly: "Are you trying to put the black on me?"

"Blackmail?" Emanuel was shocked. "There's honour amongst—friends surely, Peter. I only want what's right and fair."

Peter laughed softly, amusedly.

"Comic, is it? You can afford to laugh at a poor old fellow who's been in 'stir' for fifteen years."

The master of Manor Hill snapped round on him.

"If you'd been in hell for fifty I should still laugh."

Emanuel was sorry for himself. That was ever a weakness of his; he said as much.

"You wouldn't, would you? You've got a daughter, haven't you? Young? Married today, wasn't she?"

"Yes."

"Married money—a swell?"

"Yes. She married a good man."

"He doesn't know what you are, Peter?" Emanuel asked the question carelessly, and his host fixed him with a steely glance.

"No. What's the idea? Do you think you'll get forty thousand that way?"

"I've got a boy. You've never sat in a damp cell with the mists of the moor hanging on the walls and thought and thought till your heart ached? You can get people through their children." He paused. "I could get you that way."

In a second Peter Kane was towering above him, an ominous figure.

"The day my heart ached," he said slowly, "yours would not beat! You're an old man, and you're afraid of death! I can see it in your eyes. I am afraid of nothing. I'd kill you!"

Before the ferocity of voice and mien, Legge shrank farther into his chair.

"What's all this talk about killing? I only want what's fair. Fond of her, ain't you, Peter? I'll bet you are. They say that you're crazy about her. Is she pretty? I don't suppose she takes after you. Young Johnny Gray was sweet on her too. Peter, I'll get you through her—"

So far he got, and then a hand like a steel clamp fell on his neck, and he was jerked from his chair.

Peter spoke no word but, dragging the squirming figure behind him, as if it had neither weight nor resistance, he strode up the narrow pathway by the side of the house, across the strip of garden, through the gate and into the road. A jerk of his arm, and Emanuel Legge was floundering in the dusty road.

"Don't come back, Emanuel," he said, and did not stop to listen to the reply.

* * * *

John Gray passed out of sight and hearing of the two men, being neither curious to know Legge's business nor anxious to renew a prison acquaintance.

Below the box hedge were three broad terraces, blazing with colour, blanketed with the subtle fragrance of flowers. Beyond that, a sloping meadow leading to a little river. Peter had bought his property wisely. A great cedar of Lebanon stood at the garden's edge; to the right, massed bushes were patched with purple and heliotrope blooms.

He sat down on a marble seat, glad of the solitude which he shared only with a noisy thrush and a lark invisible in the blue above him.

Marney was married. That was the beginning and the end of him. But happy. He recognised his very human vanity in the instant doubt that she could be happy with anybody but him.

How dear she was! And then a voice came to him, a shrill, hateful voice. It was Legge's—he was threatening the girl, and Johnny's blood went cold. Here was the vulnerable point in Peter Kane's armour; the crevice through which he could be hurt.

He started to his feet and went up the broad steps of the terrace three at a time. The garden was empty, save for Barney setting a table. Kane and his guest had disappeared. He was crossing the lawn when he saw something white shining in the gloom beyond the open French windows of a room. Something that took glorious shape. A girl in bridal white, and her hands were outstretched to him. So ethereal, so unearthly was her beauty, that at first he did not recognise her.

"Johnny!"

A soldierly figure was at her side, Peter Kane was behind her, but he had no eyes for any but Marney.

She came flying toward him, both his hands were clasped in her warm palm.

"Oh, Johnny… Johnny!"

Then he looked up into the smiling face of the bridegroom, that fine, straight man to whom Peter had entrusted his beloved girl. For a second their eyes met, the debonair Major Floyd and his. Not by a flicker of eyelash did Johnny Gray betray himself.

The husband of the woman he loved was Jeff Legge, forger and traitor, the man sworn with his father to break the heart of Peter Kane.

CHAPTER 4

Had he betrayed himself, he wondered? All his will power was exercised to prevent such a betrayal Though a tornado of fury swept through and through him, though he saw the face of the man distorted and blurred, and brute instinct urged his limbs to savage action, he remained outwardly unmoved It was impossible for the beholder to be sure whether he had paled, for the sun and wind of Dartmoor had tanned his lean face the colour of mahogany For a while so terrific was the shock that he was incapable of speech or movement

"Major Floyd" was Jeff Legge! In a flash he realised the horrible plot. This was Emanuel's revenge—to marry his crook son to the daughter of Peter Kane.

Jeff was watching him narrowly, but by no sign did Johnny betray his recognition. It was all over in a fraction of a second. He brought his eyes back to the girl, smiling mechanically. She seemed oblivious to her surroundings. That her new husband stood by, watching her with a gleam of amusement in his eyes, that Peter was frowning anxiously, and that even old Barney was staring open-mouthed, meant nothing.

"Johnny, poor Johnny! You aren't hating me, are you?"

John smiled and patted the hand that lay in his.

"Are you happy?" he asked in a low voice.

"Yes, oh yes, I'm happily married—that's what you mean, isn't it? I'm very happy… Johnny, was it terrible? I haven't stopped thinking about you, I haven't. Though I didn't write… after… Don't you think I was a beast…? I know I was. Johnny, didn't it hurt you, old boy?"

He shook his head.

"There's one thing you mustn't be in Dartmoor—sorry for yourself. Are you happy?"

She did not meet his eyes.

"That is twice you've asked in a minute! Isn't it disloyal to say that I am? Don't you want to meet Jeffrey?"

"Why, of course, I want to meet Jeffrey."

He crossed to the man, and Jeff Legge watched him.

"I want you to meet Captain Gray, a very old friend of mine," she said with a catch in her voice.

Jeffrey Legge's cold hand gripped his.

"I'm glad to meet you, Captain Gray."

Had he been recognised? Apparently not, for the face turned to him was puckered in an embarrassed smile.

"You've just come back from East Africa, haven't you? Get any shooting?"

"No, I didn't do any shooting," said Johnny.

"Lots of lions, aren't there?" said Jeff.

The lips of the ex-convict twitched.

"In that part of the country where I was living, the lions are singularly tame," he said dryly.

"Marney, darling, you're glad to see Gray on your wedding day, aren't you?—it was good of you to come, Gray. Mrs. Floyd has often spoken about you."

He put his arm about the girl, his eyes never leaving Johnny's face. He designed to hurt—to hurt them both. She stood rigidly, neither yielding nor resisting, tense, breathless, pale. She knew! The realisation came to John Gray like a blow. She knew that this man was a liar and a villain. She knew the trick that had been played upon her father!

"Happy, darling?"

"Very—oh, very."

There was a flutter in her voice, and now Johnny was hurt, and the fight to hold himself in became terrific. It was Peter who for the moment saved the situation.

"Johnny, I want you to know this boy. The best in the world. And I want you to think with me that he's the best husband in the world for Marney."

Jeff Legge laughed softly.

"Mr. Kane, you embarrass me terribly. I'm not half good enough for her—I'm just an awkward brute that doesn't deserve my good luck."

He bent and kissed the white-faced girl. Johnny did not take his eyes from the man.

"Happy, eh? I'll bet you're happy, you rascal," chuckled Kane.

Marney pulled herself away from the encircling arm.

"Daddy, I don't think this is altogether amusing Johnny." Her voice shook. The man from Dartmoor knew that she was on the verge of tears.

"It takes a lot to bore me." John Gray found his voice. "Indeed, the happiness of young people—I feel very old just now—is a joy. You're a Canadian, Major Floyd?"

"Yes—a French Canadian, though you wouldn't guess that from my name. My people were *habitant* and went west in the 'sixties—to Alberta and Saskatchewan, long before the railway came. You ought to go to Canada; you'd like it better than the place you've been to."

"I'm sure I should."

Peter had strolled away, the girl's arm in his.

"No lions in Canada, tame or wild," said Jeff, regarding him from under his drooped eyelids.

Gray had lit a cigarette. He was steady now, steady of nerve and hand.

"I should feel lonely without lions," he said coolly, and then: "If you will forgive my impertinence, Major Floyd, you have married a very nice girl."

"The very, very best."

"I would go a long way to serve her—a long way. Even back to the lions."

Their eyes met. In the bridegroom's was a challenge; in Johnny Gray's cold murder. Jeff Legge's eyes fell and he shivered.

"I suppose you like—hunting?" he said. "Oh, no, you said you didn't. I wonder why a man of your—er—character went abroad?"

"I was sent," said Johnny, and he emphasised every word. "Somebody had a reason for sending me abroad—they wanted me out of the way. I should have gone, anyhow, but this man hurried the process."

"Do you know who it was?"

The East African pretence had been tacitly dropped. Jeff might do so safely, for he would know that the cause of John Gray's retirement from the world was no secret.

"I don't know the man. He was a stranger to me. Very few people know him personally. In his set—our set—not half a dozen people could identify him. Only one man in the police knows him—"

"Who is that?" interrupted the other quickly.

"A man named Reeder. I heard that in prison—of course you knew I had come from Dartmoor?"

Jeff nodded with a smile.

"That is the fellow who is called The Great Unknown," he said, striving to thin the contempt from his voice. "I've heard about him in the club. He is a very stupid person of middle age, who lives in Peckham. So he isn't as much unknown as *your* mystery man!"

"It is very likely," said the other. "Convicts invest their heroes and enemies with extraordinary gifts and qualities. I only know what I have been told. At Dartmoor they say Reeder knows everything. The Government gave him carte blanche to find the Big Printer—"

"And has he found him?" asked Jeff Legge innocently.

"He'll find him," said Johnny. "Sooner or later there will be a squeak."

"May I be there to hear it," said Jeff Legge, and showed his white teeth in a mirthless smile.

CHAPTER 5

Johnny was alone in the lower garden, huddled up on a corner of the marble bench, out of sight but not out of hearing of the guests who were assembling on the lawn He had to think, and think quickly Marney knew! But Marney had not told, and Johnny guessed why

When had Jeff Legge told her? On the way back from the church, perhaps. She would not let Peter know—Peter, who believed her future assured, her happiness beyond question. What had Jeff said? Not much, Johnny guessed. He had given her just a hint that the charming Major Floyd she had known was not the Major Floyd with whom she was to live.

Johnny was cool now—icy cold was a better description. He must be sure, absolutely sure, beyond any question of doubt. There might be some resemblance between Jeff Legge and this Major Floyd. He had only seen the crook once, and that at a distance.

He heard the rustle of skirts and looked round quickly. It was the maid he had seen quarrelling with Barney.

"Mr. Kane says, would you care to be in the group that is being photographed, Captain Gray?" she asked.

He did not immediately reply. His eyes were scanning her with a new interest.

"Tell him I'd rather not, and come back."

"Come back, sir?" she repeated in astonishment.

"Yes, I want to talk to you," said Johnny with a smile. "Have mercy on a disgruntled guest, who can find nobody to entertain him."

She stood, hesitating. He could see the indecision in her face.

"I don't know if Mr. Kane would like that," she said, and a smile trembled at the corner of her mouth. "Very well, I'll come back."

It was not till ten minutes later, when he judged the photograph had been taken and the guests had gone again to the house, that she appeared, demure but curious.

"Sit down," said Johnny. He threw away his cigarette and moved to the end of the stone bench.

"Don't stop smoking for me, Captain Gray," she said.

"How long have you been here?" he asked.

"With Mr. Kane? About six months," she said.

"Pretty good job?" he asked carelessly.

"Oh, yes, sir, very."

"What is your name?"

"My name is Lila. Why do you ask?"

"I think you and I ought to get better acquainted, Lila," he said, and took her unresisting hand.

Secretly she was amused; on the surface she showed some sign of being shocked.

"I didn't know you were that type of flirting man, Mr. Gray—you're a Captain, though, aren't you?"

"'Captain' is a purely honorary title, Lila," said Johnny. "I suppose you'll miss your lady?"

"Yes, I shall miss her," said Lila.

"A nice girl, eh?" bantered Johnny.

"And a very nice husband," she said tartly.

"Do you think so?"

"Yes, I suppose he is a nice fellow. I don't know much about him."

"Good-looking?" suggested Johnny.

The woman shrugged her shoulders.

"I suppose he is."

"And very much in love with Miss Kane. That fellow adores her," said Johnny. "In fact, I don't know that I've ever seen a man so much in love with a woman."

She suppressed a sigh.

"Oh, yes, I suppose he is," she said impatiently. "Do you want me any more, Captain Gray, because I've a lot of work to do?"

"Don't run away," said Johnny in his most gentle voice. "Weddings always make me romantic." He took up the thread where it was interrupted. "I don't expect the Major will have eyes for any other girl for years," he said. "He's head over heels in love, and why shouldn't he be? I suppose," he said reminiscently, avoiding her eyes, "he is the sort of man who would have had many love affairs in the past." He shrugged his shoulders. "With the kind of girls that one picks up and puts down at pleasure."

Now a flush, deep and even, had come to her face, and her eyes held a peculiar brightness.

"I don't know anything about Major Floyd," she said shortly, and was rising, but his hand fell upon her arm.

"Don't run away, Lila."

"I'm not going to stay," she said with sudden vehemence. "I don't want to discuss Major Floyd or anybody else. If you want me to talk to you—"

"I want to talk to you about the honeymoon. Can't you picture them, say, on Lake Como, in a bower of roses? Can't you imagine him forgetting all that's past, all the old follies, all the old girls—?"

She wrenched her arm from his grip and stood up, and her face was deadly white.

"What are you getting at, Gray?" she asked, all the deference, all the demureness gone from her voice.

"I'm getting at you, Miss Lila Sain," he said, "and if you attempt to get away from me, I'll throttle you!"

She stared at him, her breath coming quickly.

"You're supposed to be a gentleman, too," she said.

"I'm supposed to be Johnny Gray from Dartmoor. Sit down. What's the graft, Lila?"

"I don't understand what you're talking about."

"What's the graft?" asked Johnny with deadly calm. "Jeff Legge put you here to nose the house for him, and keep him wise as to what was going on."

"I don't know Jeff Legge," she faltered.

"You're a liar," said Johnny ungently. "I know you, Lila. You run with Legge and you're a cheap squeak. I've seen you a dozen times. Who is Major Floyd?"

"Go and ask him," she said defiantly.

"Who is Major Floyd?"

The grip on her arm tightened.

"You know," she said sullenly. "It's Jeff Legge."

"Now listen, Lila. Come here." He had released her, and now he crooked his finger. "Go and blow to Jeff, and I'll squeak on you both—you understand that? I'll put Jeff just where I want him to be—there's a vacant cell at Dartmoor, anyway. That gives you a twinge, doesn't it? You're keen on Jeff?"

She did not reply.

"I'll put him where I want him to be," he repeated slowly and deliberately, "unless you do as I tell you."

"You're going to put the 'black' on him?" she said, her lips curling.

"'Black' doesn't mean anything in my young life," said Johnny. "But I tell you this, that I'll find Reeder and squeak a whole pageful unless I have my way."

"What do you want?" she asked.

"I want to know where they're going, and where they're staying. I want to know their plans for the future. Are you married to him, by any chance?"

A glance at her face gave him the answer.

"You're not? Well, you may be yet, Lila. Aren't you tired of doing his dirty work?"

"Perhaps I am and perhaps I'm not," she replied defiantly. "You can do nothing to him now, anyway, Johnny Gray. He's got your girl, and if you squeaked like a garden of birds you couldn't undo what that old God-man did this morning! Jeff's too clever for you. He'll get you, Gray—"

"If he knows," said Johnny quietly. "But if he knows, Reeder knows too. Do you get that?"

"What are you going to do?" she asked after a silence.

"I'm having one of my little jokes," said Johnny between his teeth. "A real good joke! It is starting now. I can't tell Peter, because he'd kill your young man, and I have a particular objection to Peter going to the drop. And *you* can't tell Jeff, because there'd be a case for a jury, and when Jeff came out you'd be an old woman. That's not a good prospect, eh? Now tell me all you've got to tell, and speak slowly, because I don't write shorthand."

He whipped a small notebook from his pocket, and as she spoke, reluctantly, sulkily, yet fearfully, he wrote rapidly. When he had finished:

"You can go now, my gentle child," he said, and she stood up, her eyes blazing with rage.

"If you squeak, Johnny Gray, I'll kill you. I never was keen on this marriage business—naturally. I knew old Legge wanted him to marry Peter's daughter, because Legge wanted to get one back on him. But Jeff's been good to me; and the day the busies come for Legge I'll come for you, and I'll shoot you stone dead, Johnny, as God's my judge!"

"Beat it!" said Johnny tersely.

He waited till she was gone through one of the openings in the box hedge, then passed along to the other and stopped. Peter Kane was standing in the open, shielded from view by the thin box bush, and Peter's face was inscrutable.

CHAPTER 6

"Hallo, Johnny! Running for the compensation stakes?"

Johnny laughed.

"You mean the maid? She is rather pretty, isn't she?"

"Very," said the other.

Had he heard? That was a question and a fear in Johnny's mind. The marble bench was less than six feet from the bush where Peter Kane stood. If he had been there any time—

"Been waiting long for me, Peter?" he asked.

"No; I just saw you take a farewell of Lila—very nice girl, that, Johnny—an extraordinarily nice girl. I don't know when I've met a nicer. What did you find to talk about?"

"The weather, dicky-birds and the course of true love," said Johnny, as Kane took his arm and led him across the lawn.

"Everything variable and flighty, eh?" said Peter with a little smile. "Come and eat, Johnny. These people are going away soon. Marney is changing now. What do you think of my new son-in-law, eh?"

His old jovial manner held. When they came into the big reception-room and Peter Kane's arm went round his son-in-law's shoulder, Johnny breathed a sigh of relief. Thank God he did not know! He had sweated in his fear of what might follow a discovery.

Thirty-six people sat down in the dining-room, and, contrary to convention, Marney, who sat at the head of the table, was wearing her going-away dress. John shot a quick glance at her as he came in, but she averted her eyes. Her father sat on her left; next to him was the clergyman who had performed the ceremony. Next came a girl friend, and then a man, by whose side Johnny sat.

He recognised the leathery features instantly.

"Been away, Johnny?" Detective-Superintendent Craig asked the question in a voice so carefully pitched that it did not reach any farther than the man to whom he spoke.

The chatter and buzz of conversation, the little ripples of laughter that ran up and down the table, did something to make the privacy of their talk assured.

As old Barney bent over to serve a dish, Craig gave a sidelong glance at his companion.

"Peter's got old Barney still—keeping honest, Barney?"

"I'm naturally that way," said Barney *sotto voce*. "It's not meeting policemen that keeps me straight."

The hard features of the detective relaxed.

"There are lots of other people who could say that, Barney," he said, and when the man had passed to the next guest: "He's all right. Barney never was a bad man. I think he only did one stretch—he wouldn't have done that if he'd had Peter's imagination, Johnny."

"Peter's imagination?"

"I'm not referring to his present imagination, but the gift he had fourteen—fifteen years ago. Peter was the cleverest of them all. The brilliant way his attack was planned, the masterly line of retreat, the wonderful alibis, so beautifully dovetailed into one another that, if we had pinched him, he'd not only have been discharged, but he would have got something from the poor box! It used to be the life ambition of every young officer to catch him, to find some error of judgment, some flaw in his plan. But it was police-proof and fool-proof."

"He'd blush to hear you," said the other dryly.

"But it's true, Johnny! The clever letters he used to write, all to fool us. He did a lot of work with letters—getting people together, luring 'em to the place he wanted 'em and where their presence served him best. I remember how he got my chief to be at Charing Cross under the clock at ten-past nine, and showed up himself and made him prove his alibi!" He laughed gently.

"I suppose," said Gray, "people would think it remarkable that you and he are such good friends?"

"They wouldn't say it was remarkable; they'd say it was damned suspicious!" growled the other. "Having a drink?" he said suddenly, and pulled a wine bottle across the table.

"No, thanks—I seldom drink. We have to keep a very clear head in our business. We can't afford to dream."

"We can't afford anything else," said Craig. "Why 'our business,' old man? You're out of that?"

Johnny saw the girl look toward him. It was only a glance—but in that brief flash he saw all that he feared to see—the terror, the bewilderment, the helplessness. He set his teeth and turned abruptly to the detective.

"How is *your* business?" he asked.

"Quiet."

"I'm sorry to hear that," said John Gray with mock concern. "But trade's bad everywhere, isn't it?"

"What sort of time did you have—in the country?" asked Craig, and his companion grinned.

"Wonderful! My bedroom wanted papering, but the service was quite good."

Craig sighed.

"Ah well, we live and learn," he said heavily. "I was sorry about it, Johnny, very sorry. It's a misfortune, but there's no use grieving about it. You were one of the unlucky ones. If all the people who deserved prison were *in* prison—why, there wouldn't be any housing problems. I hear there were quite a lot of stars there," Craig went on. "Harry Becker, and young Lew Storing—why, old Legge must have been there in your time. And another fellow—now, what's his name? The slush man—ah, Carper, that's it. Ever see him?"

"Yes; he and I were once harnessed to the same cart."

"Ah!" said Craig encouragingly. "I'll bet you heard a few things. He'd talk to you."

"He did."

Craig bent toward him, lowering his voice.

"Suppose I told you a certain party coppered you, and suppose I said I've reason to believe that your copper is the man I want. Now couldn't we exchange confidences?" he asked.

"Yes, we might squeak together, and it would sound like one of those syncopated orchestras. But we won't. Honestly, Craig, I can't tell you about the Big Printer. Reeder ought to know all about him!"

"Reeder!" said the other scornfully. "An amateur! All this fal-de-lal about secret service men gets my goat! If they'd left the matter to the police, we'd have had the Big Printer—ever seen him, Johnny?"

"No," said Johnny untruthfully.

"Reeder, eh?" said the thoughtful detective. "They used to have an office man named Golden once, an old fellow that thought he could catch slushers by sitting in an office and thinking hard. Reeder isn't much better by all accounts. I saw him once, a soft fellow on the edge of senile decay!"

Craig sighed deeply, looked up and down the happy board with a bleak and grudging glance, and then:

"Just for a little heart-to-heart talk, I know where you could get an easy 'monkey,'[*£500] Johnny," he said softly.

Johnny did not smile.

"It would have to be a monkey on a stick, Craig—"

"We're both men of the world," interrupted the detective imploringly.

"Yes," said Johnny Gray, "but not the same world, Craig."

One last despairing effort the detective made, though he knew that, in angling for a squeak, he might as well have tried Peter himself.

"The Bank of England will pay a thousand pounds for the information I want."

"And who can afford it better?" said Johnny heartily. "Now, shut up, Craig; somebody's going to make a speech."

It was a mild and beatific oration delivered by the officiating clergyman. When it came to its machine-made peroration Craig, who was intensely interested in the sonorous platitudes, looked round and saw that his companion had gone from his side—later he saw him leaning over Peter's chair, and Peter was nodding vigorously. Then Johnny passed through the door.

Somebody else was watching him. The bridegroom, twiddling the stem of his wineglass between his fingers, saw him go, and was more than ordinarily interested. He was sufficiently curious, at any rate, to catch the eye of the pretty maid and look significantly at the door. At that signal Lila followed Johnny Gray. He was not in the hall, and she went out into the road, but here saw no sign of the man she sought. There was, however, somebody else, and she obeyed his call to her.

"Tell Jeff I want him before he starts on that honeymoon of his," snarled Emanuel Legge, glaring at her through the glasses. "He's been talking to that girl—I saw her face. What did he say?"

"How do I know?" she snapped back. "You and your Jeff! I wish to the Lord I'd never come into this job. What's the graft, anyway? That flash crook knows all about it, Legge."

"Who—Johnny Gray? Is he here? He did come, then?"

She nodded.

"What do you mean—'he knows'?"

"He knows Jeff—recognised him first pop," said the girl inelegantly, and Emanuel Legge whistled.

"Have you told Jeff that he has been recognised?"

The harsh features of Emanuel Legge were drawn and tense.

"What is the use of asking me? I haven't had a word with him. He's so taken up with this girl—"

"Forget it," said Legge with a gesture. "Tell me what this Johnny Gray says."

"I'll tell you one thing that amused me," said the girl grimly. "He said he'd throttle me if I squeaked! And he's got a fascinating pair of hands. I shouldn't like to play rough with that fellow—there's no use in tut-tutting me, Emanuel. I've told you all he said. He knows Jeff; he must have seen him before he went 'over the Alps.'"

The old man was thinking, his brow furrowed, his lips pursed.

"It's pretty bad if he guesses, because he's sweet on the girl, and there's going to be trouble. Get Jeff out quick!"

"If you stay here, Peter will see you," she warned him. "Go down the lane and turn into the private path. I'll send Jeff to you in the lower garden."

Nodding, he hurried away. It took her some time to find an opportunity, but presently she signalled the man with her eyes, and he followed her to the lawn.

"The old man's waiting down in the lower garden," she said in a low voice. "Hurry."

"What is wrong?" he asked quickly, sensing trouble.

"He'll tell you."

With a glance round Jeff hurried on to the terrace just as his father reached the rendezvous.

"Jeff, Gray knows."

The man drew a quick breath.

"Me?" he said incredulously. "He didn't so much as bat a lid when I met him."

Emanuel nodded.

"That fellow's hell cool—the most dangerous crook in the world. I was in the Awful Place with him, and I know his reputation. There's nothing he's afraid of. If he tells Peter... shoot first! Peter won't be carrying a gun, but he's sure to have one within travelling distance—and Peter is a quick mover. I'll cover you; I've got two boys handy that 'mind' me, and Johnny... well, he'll get what's coming."

"What am I to do?"

Jeff Legge was biting his nails thoughtfully.

"Get the girl away—you're due to leave by car, ain't you? Get her to the Charlton Hotel. You're supposed to stay there a week—make it a day. Clear to Switzerland tomorrow and stop her writing. I'll fix Peter. He'll pay."

"For what?"

"To get his girl back; forty thousand—maybe more."

Jeff Legge whistled.

"I didn't see that side of the graft before. It's a new variety of 'black.'"

"It's what I choose to call it!" hissed his father. "You're in fifty-fifty. You can have the lot so far as I care. *You make that girl eat dirt*, d'ye hear? Put her right down to earth, Jeff.... Peter will pay."

"I promised Lila..." began the other, hesitant.

"Promise your Aunt Rebecca Jane!" Emanuel almost screamed. "Lila! That trash, and you the big man, too—what are ye running? A girls' refuge society? Get!"

"What about Gray?"

"I'll fix Gray!"

CHAPTER 7

The old man made his way back to the road and passed quickly along until he came to the main highway Two men were seated in the shade of a bush, eating bread and cheese They came quickly enough when he whistled them, tall, broad-shouldered men whose heavy jowls had not felt a lather-brush for days

"Either of you boys know Johnny Gray?" he asked.

"I was on the 'moor' with him," said one gruffly, "if he's the fellow that went down for 'ringing in' horses?"

Emanuel nodded.

"He's in the house, and it's likely he'll walk to the station, and likely enough take the short cut across the fields. That'll be easy for you. He's got to be coshed—you understand? Get him good, even if you have to do it in the open. If there's anybody with him, get him in London. But get him."

Emanuel came back to his observation post as the first of the cars went into the drive. Jeff was moving quickly—and there was need.

Presently the car came out. Emanuel caught a glimpse of Jeff and the frightened face of the girl, and rubbed his hands in an ecstasy of satisfaction. Peter was standing in the middle of the road, watching the car. If he knew! The smile vanished from the old man's face. Peter did not know; he had not been told. Why? Johnny would not let her go, knowing. Perhaps Lila was lying. You can never trust women of that kind; they love sensation. Johnny… dangerous. The two words left one impression. And there was Johnny, standing, one hand in pocket, the other waving at the car as it came into brief view on the Shoreham road, as unconcerned as though he were the least interested.

A second car went in and came out. Some guests were leaving. Now, if Johnny had sense, he would be driven to London with a party. But Johnny hadn't sense. He was just a poor sucker, like all cheap crooks are. He came out alone, crossed the road and went down the narrow passage that led to the field path.

Emanuel looked backward. His bulldogs had seen and were moving parallel to the unconscious Gray.

From the road two paths led to the field, forming a Y where they met. Johnny had passed the fork when he heard the footsteps behind him. Glancing back, he saw a familiar face and did some shrewd guessing. He could run and easily outdistance these clumsy men. He preferred to face them, and turned, holding his malacca cane in both hands.

"'Lo, Gray," said the bigger of the men. "Where'n thunder are you going in such a hurry? I want to talk with you, you dirty squeaker! You're the fellow that told the deputy I was getting tobacco in through a screw!"

It was a crude invention, but good enough to justify the rough house that was booked to follow. They carried sticks in their hands, pliable canes, shotted at the end.

The blow missed Johnny as he stepped back, and then something long and bright glittered in the afternoon sun. The scabbard of the sword cane he held defensively before him, the sword, thin and deadly, was pointed to the nearer of his enemies. They stopped, Saxon-like, appalled by the sight of steel.

"Bad boy!" said Johnny reproachfully.

The razor-pointed rapier flickered from face to face, and the men stumbled back, getting into one another's way. One of the men felt something wet on his cheek, and put up his hand. When it came down it was wet and red.

"Beast, you have my brand!" said Johnny with deadly pleasantry. "Come when I call you."

He clicked the sword back in its wooden sheath and strode away. His indifference, his immense superiority, was almost as tremendously impressive as his cold toleration.

"He's ice, that fellow," said the man with the cut cheek. A sob of rage softened the rasp of his voice. "By… I'll kill him for that!"

But he made no attempt to follow, and his companion was glad.

John Gray increased his pace, and after a while emerged into the outskirts of the town. Here he found a Ford cab and reached the station in time to see the train pull out. He had made a mistake; the time-table had been changed that day, but in half an hour there was a fast train from Brighton that stopped only at Horsham.

He crossed the station yard to an hotel and was in the telephone booth for a quarter of an hour before he emerged, his collar limp, perspiration streaming down his face.

There was no sign of a familiar face when he came back to the platform. He expected to see Emanuel eventually, and here he was not disappointed, for Emanuel arrived a few minutes before the Brighton train came in.

Officially, it was their first meeting since they had been members of the same farm gang at Dartmoor, and Legge's expression of surprise was therefore appropriate.

"Why, if it isn't Gray! Well, fancy meeting you, old man! Well, this is a surprise! When did you come out?"

"Cease your friendly badinage," said Johnny shortly. "If we can get an empty compartment, I've got a few words to say to you, Emanuel."

"Been down to the wedding?" asked the old man slyly. "Nice girl, eh? Done well for herself? They tell me he's a Canadian millionaire. Ain't that

Peter's luck! That fellow would fall off rock and drop in feathers, he's that lucky."

Johnny made no answer. When the train stopped and he found himself opposite a first-class carriage, he opened the door and Emanuel hopped in.

"If you're short of money—" began Legge.

"I'm not," said the other curtly. "I'm short of nothing except bad company. Now listen, Emanuel"—the train was puffing slowly from the station when he spoke again—"I'm going to give you a chance."

The wide-eyed astonishment of Emanuel Legge was very convincing, but Johnny was not open to conviction at the moment.

"I don't get you, Johnny," he said. "What's all this talk about giving me a chance? Have you been drinking?"

Johnny had seated himself opposite the man, and now he leant forward and placed his hand upon the other's knee.

"Emanuel," he said gently, "call off that boy, and there'll be no squeak. Take that wounded fawn look from your face, because I haven't any time for fooling. You call off Jeff and send the girl back home tonight, or I squeak. Do you understand that?"

"I understand your words, Johnny Gray, but what they mean is a mystery to me." Emanuel Legge shook his head. "What boy are you talking about? I've only got one boy, and he's at college—"

"You're a paltry old liar. I'm talking about Jeff Legge, who married Peter's daughter today. I've tumbled to your scheme, Emanuel. You're getting even with Peter. Well, get even with him, but try some other way."

"She's married him of her own free will," began the man. "There's no law against that, is there, Johnny? Fell in love with him right on the spot! That's what I like to see, Johnny—young people in love."

If he hoped to rattle his companion he was disappointed.

"Now he can unmarry of his own free will," said Johnny calmly. "Listen to me, Emanuel Legge. When you arrive in London, you'll go straight away to the Charlton Hotel and talk very plainly to your son. He, being a sensible man, will carry out your instructions—"

"*Your* instructions," corrected Emanuel, his mouth twisted in a permanent smile. "And what happens if I don't, Johnny?"

"I squeak," said Johnny, and the smile broadened.

"They are married, old man. You can't divorce 'em. You can turn a brown horse into a black 'un, but you can't turn Mrs. Jeffrey Legge into Miss Marney Kane, clever as you are."

Johnny leant forward.

"I can turn Mr. Jeffrey Legge into Dartmoor Jail," he said unpleasantly, "and that's what I propose to do."

"On what charge?" Emanuel raised his eyebrows. "Give us a little rehearsal of this squeal of yours, Gray."

"He's the Big Printer," said Johnny, and the smile slowly dissolved. "The Government has spent thousands to catch him; they've employed the best secret service men in the world to pull him down, and I can give them just the information they want. I know where his stuff is planted. I know where it is printed; I know at least four of his agents. You think Jeff's secret is his own and yours, but you're mistaken, Emanuel. Craig knows he's the Big Printer; he told me so at lunch. All he wants is evidence, and the evidence I can give him. Old Reeder knows—you think he's a fool, but he knows. I could give him a squeak that would make him the cleverest lad in the world."

Emanuel Legge licked his dry lips.

"Going in for the 'con.' business, Johnny?" he asked banteringly. There was no amusement in his voice. "What a confidence man you'd make! You look like a gentleman, and talk like one. Why, they'd fall for you and never think twice! But that confidence stuff doesn't mean anything to me, Johnny. I'm too old and too wide to be bluffed—"

"There's no bluff here," interrupted Johnny. "I have got your boy like that!" He held out his hand and slowly clenched it.

For fully five minutes Emanuel Legge sat huddled in a corner of the compartment, staring out upon the flying scenery.

"You've got him like that, have you, Johnny boy?" he said gently. "Well, there's no use deceiving you, I can see. Slush is funny stuff—they call it phoney' in America. Did you know that? I guess you would, because you're well educated. But it's good slush, Johnny. Look at this. Here's a note. Is it good or bad?"

His fingers had gone into his waistcoat pocket and withdrew a thin pad of paper an inch square. Fold by fold he opened it out and showed a five-pound note. He caressed the paper with finger and thumb. The eyes behind the powerful glasses gleamed; the thin-lined face softened with pride.

"Is it good or bad, Johnny?"

Though the day was bright and hot, and not a cloud was in the sky, the four electric lamps in the carriage lit up suddenly. In the powerful light of day they seemed pale ghosts of flame, queerly dim. As the sunshine fell upon them their shadows were cast upon the white cornice of the carriage.

"There's a tunnel coming," said Emanuel. "It will give you a chance of seeing them at their best—feel 'em, Johnny! The real paper; bankers have fallen for 'em...."

With a roar the train plunged into the blackness of the tunnel. Emanuel stood with his back to the carriage door, the note held taut between his hands.

"There's only one flaw—the watermark. I'm giving away secrets, eh? Look!"

He stretched his arms up until he held the note against one of the bracket lamps. To see, John Gray had to come behind him and peer over his shoulder. The thunder of the train in the narrow tunnel was almost deafening.

"Look at the 'F'," shouted Emanuel. "See… that 'F' in 'Five'—it's printed too shallow…."

As Johnny bent forward the old man thrust at him with his shoulder, and behind that lurch of his was all the weight and strength of his body. Taken by surprise, John Gray was thrown from his balance. He staggered back against the carriage door, felt it give, and tried to recover his equilibrium. But the thrust was too well timed. The door flew open, and he dropped into the black void, clutching as he did so the window ledge. For a second he swayed with the in and out swinging of the door. Then Legge's clenched fist hammered down on his fingers, and he dropped….

CHAPTER 8

He struck a layer of thick sand and turned a complete somersault The wall of the tunnel caught and almost dislocated his arm, and he rebounded toward the whirling wheels One wheel flicked him back against the wall, and he slid, his arms covering his face, the flint ballast of the road ripping his sleeves to ribbons…

He was alive. The train had passed. He saw the red tail-lights closing to one another. Gingerly he moved first one leg and then the other; then he rolled over toward the wall and lay on his back without further movement. His heart was pounding furiously; he felt a soreness working through the numb overlay of shock. Shock… shock sometimes killed men. His heart was going faster yet; he experienced a horrible nausea, and he found himself trembling violently.

The proper thing to do was to inject a solution of gum-acacia into his veins (his thoughts were curiously well ordered). Doctors did that; he remembered the doctor telling him at Dartmoor.

But there was no gum-acacia to be had…. Ten minutes later he lifted his body on his elbow and struggled to a sitting position. His head swam, but it did not ache; his arms… he felt them carefully. They were very sore, but no bones were broken.

A roadman at the exit of the tunnel nearly dropped with amazement as a grimy young man whose clothes were in rags emerged, limping.

"I fell out," said Johnny. "Can you tell me if there is anywhere I can hire a car?"

The roadman was going off duty and was willing to act as guide. Johnny hobbled up the steep slopes of the railway cutting, and with the assistance of the interested workman, traversed a wide field to the road. And then came a blessed sportsman on his way back from Gatwick Races, and he was alone in his car.

At first he looked suspicious at the bruised and ragged figure that had held him up. In the end he flung open the door by his side.

"Step up," he said.

To the railway worker Johnny had a few words to say.

"Here's five," he said. "Two for your help and three to stop your talking. I don't want this business to be reported, you understand? The truth is, I had been looking on the wine when it was red and gaveth its colour aright."

Johnny had evidently touched a sympathetic chord.

"You mean you was boozed?" said the man. "You can trust me."

The angel who drove him to London was not a talkative angel. Beyond expressing the wish that something drastic had happened to *him* before he went racing, and the advancement of his view that all racing was crooked and all jockeys thieves, he contributed little to the entertainment of his passenger, and the passenger was glad.

At the first cab-rank they struck—it was in Sutton—Johnny insisting upon alighting.

"I'll take you home if you like," said his gloomy benefactor.

Gently the other declined.

"My name is Lawford," said the motorist in a sudden outburst of confidence. "I've got an idea I know your face. Haven't I seen you on the track?"

"Not for some time," said Johnny.

"Rather like a fellow I once met... well, introduced to... fellow named Gay or Gray... regular rascal. He got time."

"Thanks," said Johnny, "that was I!" and the hitherto reticent Mr. Lawford became almost conversational in his apologies.

The young man finished the journey in a Sutton taxi and reached Queen's Gate late in the afternoon.

Parker, who opened the door to him, asked no questions.

"I have laid out another suit for you, sir," he returned to the study to say—the only oblique reference he made to his employer's disorder.

As he lay in a hot bath, soaking the stiffness out of his limbs, Johnny examined his injuries. They were more or less superficial, but he had had a terribly narrow escape from death, and he was not wholly recovered from the violence of it. Emanuel had intended his destruction. The attempt did not surprise him. Men of Legge's type worked that way. He met them in Dartmoor. They would go to a killing without fire of rage or frenzy of despair. Once he had seen a convict select with deliberation and care a large jagged stone and drop it upon the head of a man working in the quarry below. Fortunately, a warder had seen the act, and his shout saved the intended victim from mutilation. The assailant had only one excuse. The man he had attacked had slighted him in some way.

In the hearts of these men lived a cold beast. Johnny often pictured it, an obscene shape with pale, lidless eyes and a straight slit of a mouth. He had seen the beast staring at him from a hundred distorted faces, had heard its voice, had seen its hatefulness expressed in actions that he shivered to recall. Something of the beast had saturated into his own soul.

When he came from his bath, the masseur whom Parker had summoned was waiting, and for half an hour he groaned under the kneading hands.

The evening newspaper that Parker procured contained no news of the "accident"—Emanuel was hardly likely to report the matter, even for his own protection. There were explanations he could offer—Johnny thought of several.

Free from the hands of the masseur, he rested in his dressing-gown.

"Has anybody called?" he asked.

"A Mr. Reeder, sir."

Johnny frowned.

"Mr. Reeder?" he repeated. "What did he want?"

"I don't know, sir. He merely asked for you. A middle-aged man, with rather a sad face," said Parker. "I told him you were not at home, and that I would take any message for you, but he gave none."

His employer made no reply. For some reason, the call of the mysterious Mr. Reeder worried him more than the memory of the tragic happening of that afternoon, more, for the moment, than the marriage of Marney Kane.

CHAPTER 9

Marney made her journey to London that afternoon in almost complete silence She sat in a corner of the limousine, and felt herself separated from the man she had married by a distance which was becoming immeasurable Once or twice she stole a timid glance at him, but he was so preoccupied with his thoughts that he did not even notice They were not pleasant thoughts, to judge by his unchanging scowl All the way up he nibbled at his nails; a wrinkle between his eyes

It was not until the big car was bowling across one of the river bridges that the strain was relieved, and he turned his head, regarding her coldly.

"We're going abroad tomorrow," he said, and her heart sank.

"I thought you were staying in town for a week, Jeff," she asked, trouble in her eyes. "I told father—"

"Does it matter?" he said roughly, and then she found courage to ask him a question that had been in her mind during that dreary ride.

"Jeff, what did you mean this morning, on the way back from the church…? You frightened me."

Jeff Legge chuckled softly.

"I frightened you, did I?" he sneered. "Well, if that's all that's going to happen to you, you're a lucky girl!"

"But you're so changed…" she was bewildered. "I—I didn't want to marry you… I thought you wanted… and father was so very anxious…"

"Your father was very anxious that you should marry a man in good society with plenty of money," he said, emphasising every word. "Well, you've married him, haven't you? When I told you this morning that I'd got your father like that"—he put out his thumb suggestively—"I meant it. I suppose you know your father's a crook?"

The beautiful face flushed and went pale again.

"How dare you say that?" she asked, her voice trembling with anger. "You know it isn't true. You know!"

Jeffrey Legge closed his eyes wearily.

"There's a whole lot of revelations coming to you, my good girl," he said, "but I guess we'd better wait till we reach the hotel."

Silence followed, until the car drew up before the awning of the Charlton, and then Jeff became his smiling, courteous self, and so remained until the door of their sitting-room closed upon them.

"Now, you've got to know something, and you can't know it too soon," he said, throwing his hat upon a settee. "My name isn't Floyd at all. I'm Jeffrey Legge. My father was a convict until six months ago. He was put in prison by Peter Kane."

She listened, open-mouthed, stricken dumb with amazement and fear.

"Peter Kane is a bank robber—or he was till fifteen years ago, when he did a job with my father, got away with a million dollars, and squeaked on his pal."

"Squeaked?" she said, bewildered.

"Your father betrayed him," said Jeffrey patiently. "I'm surprised that Peter hasn't made you acquainted with the technical terms of the business. He squeaked on his pal, and my father went down for twenty years."

"It is not true," she said indignantly. "You are inventing this story. My father was a broker. He never did a dishonest thing in his life. And if he had, he would never have betrayed his friend!"

The answer seemed to amuse Legge.

"Broker, was he? I suppose that means he's a man who's broken into strong-rooms? That's the best joke I've heard for a long time! Your father's crook! Johnny knows he's crook. Craig knows he's crook. Why in hell do you think a broker should be a pal of a busy.' And take that look off your face—a busy' is a detective. Peter has certainly neglected your education!"

"Johnny knows?" she said, horror-stricken. "Johnny knows father is—I don't believe it! All you have told me is lies. If it were so, why should you want to marry me?"

Suddenly she realised the truth, and stood, frozen with horror, staring back at the smiling man.

"You've guessed, eh? We've been waiting to get under Peter's skin for years. And I guess we've got there. And now, if you like, you can tell him. There's a telephone; call him up. Tell him I'm Jeff Legge, and that all the wonderful dreams he has had of seeing you happy and comfortable are gone! Phone him! Tell him you never wanted to marry me, and it was only to make him happy that you did—you've got to break his heart, anyway. You might as well start now."

"He'd kill you," she breathed.

"Maybe he would. And that'd be a fine idea too. We'd have Peter on the trap. It would be worth dying for. But I guess he wouldn't kill me. At the sight of a gun in his hands, I'd shoot him like a dog. But don't let that stop you telling him, Marney darling."

He stretched out his hand, but she recoiled from him in horror and loathing.

"You planned it all… this was your revenge?"

He nodded.

"But Johnny… Johnny doesn't know."

She saw the change in the man's face, that suave assurance of his vanish. "He does know." She pointed an accusing finger at him. "He knows!"

"He knows, but he let you go, honey," said Jeff. "He's one of us, and we never squeak. One of us!" he repeated the words mechanically.

She sat down and covered her face with her hands, and Jeffrey, watching her, thought at first that she was crying. When she raised her face, her eyes were dry. And, more extraordinary to him the fear that he had seen was no longer there.

"Johnny will kill you," she said simply. "He wouldn't let me go… like that… if he knew. It isn't reasonable to suppose that he would, is it?"

It was Jeff Legge's turn to be uncomfortable. Not at the menace of Johnny's vengeance, but at her utter calmness. She might have been discussing the matter impartially with a third person. For a moment he lost his grip of the situation. All that she said was so obviously, so patently logical, and instinctively he looked round as though he expected to find Johnny Gray at his elbow. The absurdity of the situation struck him, and he chuckled nervously.

"Johnny!" he sneered. "What do you expect Johnny to do, eh? He's just out of 'bird'—that's jail; it is sometimes called 'boob'—I see there's a whole lot of stuff you've got to learn before you get right into the family ways."

He lounged toward her and dropped his hands on her shoulders.

"Now, old girl," he said, "there are two things you can do. You can call up Peter and put him wise, or you can make the best of a bad job."

"I'll call father," she said, springing up. Before she could reach the telephone, his arm was round her, and he had swung her back.

"You'll call nothing," he said. "There's no alternative, my little girl. You're Mrs. Legge, and I lowered myself to marry the daughter of such a squealing old hound! Marney, give me a kiss. You've not been very free with your tokens of affection, and I haven't pressed you, for fear of scaring you off. Always the considerate gentleman—that's Jeff Legge."

Suddenly she was in his arms, struggling desperately. He tried to reach her lips, but she buried her face in his coat, until, with a savage jerk that almost dislocated her shoulder, he had flung her at arm's distance. She looked up at the inflamed face and shuddered.

"I've got you, Marney." His voice was hoarse with triumph. "I've got you properly… legally. You're my wife! You realise that? No man can come between you and me."

He pulled her toward him, caught her pale face between his hands, and turned it up to his. With all the strength of utter horror and loathing, she tore herself free, fled to the door, flung it open, and stood back, wide-eyed with amazement.

In the doorway stood a tall, broad woman, with vividly red hair and a broad, good-humoured face. From her costume she was evidently one of the chambermaids of the hotel. From her voice she was most obviously Welsh.

"What are you doing here?" demanded Jeff. "Get out, damn you!"

"Why do you talk so at me now, look you? I will not have this bad language. The maid of this suite I am!"

Marney saw her chance of escaping, and, running into the room, slammed the door and locked it.

CHAPTER 10

For a moment Jeff Legge stood, helpless with rage Then he flung all his weight against the door, but it did not yield He took up the telephone, but changed his mind He did not want a scandal Least of all did he wish to be advertised as Jeffrey Legge Compromise was a blessed word—he knocked at the door

"Marney, come out and be sensible," he said. "I was only joking. The whole thing was just to try you—"

She offered no reply. There was probably a telephone in the bedroom, he thought. Would she dare call her father? He heard another door unlocked. The bedroom gave on to the corridor, and he went out, to see the big chambermaid emerging. She was alone, and no sooner was she outside the door than it was locked upon her.

"I'll report you to the management," he said furiously. He could have murdered her without compunction. But his rage made no impression upon the phlegmatic Welsh woman.

"A good character I have, look you, from all my employers. To be in the bedroom, it was my business. You shall not use bad language to me, look you, or I will have the law on you!"

Jeffrey thought quickly. He waited in the corridor until the woman had disappeared, then he beckoned from the far end a man who was evidently the floor waiter.

"Go down to the office and ask the manager, with my compliments, if I can have a second set of keys to my rooms," he said suavely. "My wife wishes to have her own."

He slipped a bill into the man's hand, of such magnitude that the waiter was overwhelmed.

"Certainly, sir. I think I can arrange," he said.

"And perhaps you would lend me your pass key," said Jeff carelessly.

"I haven't a pass key, sir. Only the management have that," replied the man; "but I believe I can get you what you want."

He came back in a few minutes to the sitting-room with many apologies. There were no duplicate sets of keys.

Jeff closed the sitting-room door on the man and locked it. Then he went over to the bedroom door.

"Marney!" he called, and this time she answered him. "Are you going to be sensible?"

"I think I'm being very sensible," was her reply.

"Come out and talk to me."

"Thank you, I would rather remain here."

There was a pause.

"If you go to your father, I will follow and kill him. I've got to shoot first, you know, Marney, after what you've told me."

There was a silence, and he knew that his words had impressed her.

"Think it over," he suggested. "Take your time about it."

"Will you promise to leave me alone?" she asked.

"Why, sure, I'll promise anything," he said, and meant it. "Come out, Marney," he wheedled. "You can't stay there all day. You've got to eat."

"The woman will bring me my dinner," was the instant reply, and Jeffrey cursed her softly.

"All right, have it your own way," he said. "But I tell you this, that if you don't come out tonight, there will be trouble in your happy family."

He was satisfied, even though she did not answer him, that Marney would make no attempt to communicate with her father—that night, at least. After that night, nothing mattered.

He got on to the telephone, but the man he sought had not arrived. A quarter of an hour later, as he was opening his second bottle of champagne, the telephone bell tinkled and Emanuel Legge's voice answered him.

"She's giving me trouble," he said in a low voice, relating what had happened.

He heard his father's click of annoyance and hastened to excuse his own precipitancy.

"She had to know sooner or later."

"You're a fool," snarled the old man. "Why couldn't you leave it?"

"You've got to cover me here," said Jeff urgently. "If she phones to Peter, there is going to be trouble. And Johnny—"

"Don't worry about Johnny," said Emanuel Legge unpleasantly. "There will be no kick coming from him."

He did not offer any explanation, and Jeff was too relieved by the assurance in his father's voice to question him on the subject.

"Take a look at the keyhole," said Emanuel, "and tell me if the key's in the lock. Anyway, I'll send you a couple of tools, and you'll open that door in two jiffs—but you've got to wait until the middle of the night, when she's asleep."

Half an hour later a small package arrived by district messenger, and Jeffrey, cutting the sealed cord, opened the little box and picked out two curiously wrought instruments. For an hour he practised on the door of the second bedroom leading from the saloon, and succeeded in turning the key from the reverse side. Toward dinner-time he heard voices in Marney's bedroom, and, creeping to the door, listened. It was the Welsh woman, and there came to his ears the clatter of plates and cutlery, and he smiled.

He had hardly got back to his chair and his newspaper when the telephone bell rang. It was the reception clerk.

"There's a lady to see you. She asked if you'd come down. She says it is very important."

"Who is it?" asked Jeffrey, frowning.

"Miss Lila."

"Lila!" He hesitated. "Send her up, please," he said, and drew a heavy velvet curtain across the door of Marney's room.

At the first sight of Peter Kane's maid he knew that she had left Horsham in a hurry. Under the light coat she wore he saw the white collar of her uniform.

"What's the trouble with you, Lila?" he asked.

"Where is Marney?" she asked.

He nodded to the curtained room.

"Have you locked her in?"

"To be exact, she locked herself in," said Jeff with a twisted smile.

The eyes of the woman narrowed.

"Oh, it's like that, is it?" she asked harshly. "You haven't lost much time, Jeff."

"Don't get silly ideas in your nut," he said coolly. "I told her who I was, and there was a row—that's all there is to it. Now, what's the trouble?"

"Peter Kane's left Horsham with a gun in his pocket—that's all," she said, and Jeffrey paled.

"Sit down and tell me just what you mean."

"After you'd gone I went up to my room because I was feeling mighty bad," she said. "I've got my feelings, and there isn't a woman breathing that can see a man go away with another girl—"

"Cut out all the sentiment and let's get right down to the facts," commanded Jeff.

"I'll tell it in my own way if you don't mind, Jeffrey Legge," said Lila.

"Well, get on with it," he said impatiently.

"I wasn't there long before I heard Peter in his room—it is underneath mine—and he was talking to himself. I guess curiosity got the better of my worry, and I went down and listened. I couldn't hear what he was saying, and so I opened the door of his room a little bit. He had just changed. The moment I went in he was slipping the magazine in the butt of a Browning—I saw him put it in his coat pocket, and then I went downstairs. After a while he came down too, and, Jeff, I didn't like the look of his face. It was all grey and pinched, and if ever I saw a devil in a man's eyes I saw it in Peter Kane's.

I heard him order the car, and then I went down into the kitchen, thinking he was going at once. But he didn't leave for about half an hour."

"What was he doing?"

"He was in his own room, writing. I don't know what he was writing, because he always uses a black blotting-pad. He must have written a lot, because I know there were half a dozen sheets of stationery in the rack, and when I went in after he'd left they had all gone. There was nothing torn up in the waste-paper basket, and he'd burnt nothing, so he must have taken all the stuff with him. I tried to get you on the phone, but you hadn't arrived, and I decided to come up."

"How did you come up—by train or car?"

"By taxi. There wasn't a train for nearly two hours."

"You didn't overtake Peter by any chance?"

She shook her head.

"I wouldn't. He was driving himself; his machine is a Spanz, and it moves!"

Jeff bit his nails.

"That gun of Peter's worries me a little," he said after a while, "because he isn't a gunman. Wait."

He took up the telephone and again called his father, and in a few words conveyed the story which Lila had brought.

"You'll have to cover me now," he said anxiously. "Peter knows."

A long pause.

"Johnny must have told him. I didn't dream he would," said Emanuel. "Keep to the hotel, and don't go out. I'll have a couple of boys watching both entrances, and if Peter shows his nose in Pall Mall he's going to be hurt."

Jeff hung up the receiver slowly and turned to the girl.

"Thank you, Lila. That's all you can do for me."

"It is not all you can do for me," said Lila. "Jeff, what is going to happen now? I've tried to pin you down, but you're a little too shifty for me. You told me that this was going to be one of those high-class platonic marriages which figure in the divorce courts, and, Jeff, I'm beginning to doubt."

"Then you're a wise woman," said Jeffrey calmly.

For a moment she did not understand the significance of the words.

"I'm a wise woman?" she repeated. "Jeff, you don't mean—"

"I'm entitled to my adventures," said Jeffrey, settling himself comfortably in the big arm-chair and crossing his legs. "I have a dear little wife, and for the moment, Lila, our little romance is finished."

"You don't mean that?" she asked unsteadily. "Jeff, you're kidding. You told me that all you wanted was to get a share of Peter's money, and Emanuel told me the same. He said he was going to put the 'black' on Peter and get away with forty thousand."

"In the meantime I've got away with the girl," said Jeffrey comfortably, "and there's no sense in kicking up a fuss, Lila. We've had a good time, and change is everything in life."

She was on her feet now, glaring down at him.

"And have I been six months doing slavey work, nosing for you, Jeffrey Legge, to be told that our little romance is finished?" she asked shrilly. "You've double-crossed me, you dirty thief! And if I don't fix you, my name's not Lila."

"It isn't," said Jeffrey. He reached for a cigar and lit it. "And never was. Your name's Jane—that is, if you haven't been telling me lies. Now, Lila, be an intelligent human being. I've put aside five hundred for you—"

"Real money, I hope," she sneered. "No, you're not going to get away with it so easy, Mr. Jeffrey Legge. You've fooled me from beginning to end, and you either carry out your promise or I'll—"

"Don't say you'll squeak," said Jeffrey, closing his eyes in mock resignation. "You're all squeakers. I'm tired of you! You don't think I'd give you anything to squeak about, do you? That I'd trust you farther than I could fling you? No, my girl, I'm four kinds of a fool, but not that kind. You know just as much about me as the police know, or as Johnny Gray knows. You can't tell my new wife, because she knows too. And Peter knows—in fact, I shouldn't be surprised if somebody didn't write a story about it in the newspapers tomorrow!"

He took out his pocket-case, opened it, and from a thick wad of notes peeled five, which he flung on to the table.

"There's your 'monkey,' and au revoir, beauteous maiden," he said.

She took up the notes slowly, folded them, and slipped them into her bag. Her eyes were burning fires, her face colourless.

If she had flown at him in a fury he would have understood, and was, in fact, prepared. But she said nothing until she stood, the knob of the door in her hand.

"There are three men after you, Jeffrey Legge," she said, "and one will get you. Reeder, or Johnny, or Peter—and if they fail, you look out for me!"

And on this threat she took her departure, slamming the door behind her, and Jeffrey settled down again to his newspaper, with the feeling of satisfaction which comes to a man who has got through a very unpleasant task.

CHAPTER 11

In a long, sedate road in suburban Brockley lived a man who had apparently no fixed occupation He was tall, thin, somewhat cadaverous, and he was known locally as a furtive night-bird Few had seen him in the day-time, and the inquisitive who, by skilful cross-examination, endeavoured to discover his business from a reticent housekeeper learnt comparatively little, and that little inaccurate Policemen on night duty, morning wayfarers had seen him walking up Brockley Road in the early hours, coming apparently from the direction of London He was known as Mr JG Reeder Letters in that name came addressed to him—large blue letters, officially stamped and sealed and in consequence it was understood in postal circles that he held a Government position

The local police force never troubled him. He was one of the subjects which it was not permissible to discuss. Until the advent of Emanuel Legge that afternoon, nobody ever remembered Mr. Reeder having a caller.

Emanuel had come from prison to the affairs of the everyday world with a clearer perception of values than his son. He was too old a criminal to be under any illusions. Sooner or later, the net of the law would close upon Jeffrey, and the immunity which he at present enjoyed would be at an end. To every graft came its inevitable lagging. Emanuel, wise in his generation, had decided upon taking the boldest step of his career. And that he did so was not flattering to the administration of justice; nor could it be regarded as a tribute to the integrity of the police.

Emanuel had "straightened" many a young detective, and not a few advanced in years. He knew the art of "dropping" to perfection. In all his life he had only met three or four men who were superior to the well-camouflaged bribe. A hundred here and there makes things easier for the big crook; a thousand will keep him out of the limelight; but, once the light is on him, not a million can disturb the inevitable march of justice. Emanuel was working in the pre-limelight stage, and hoped for success.

If his many inquiries were truthfully answered, the police had not greatly changed since his young days. Secret service men were new to him. He had thought, in spite of the enormous sums allocated to that purpose in every year's budget, that secret service was an invention of the sensational novelist; and even now, he imagined Mr. Reeder to be one who was subsidised from the comparatively private resources of the banks rather than from the Treasury.

It was Emanuel's action to grasp the nettle firmly. "In-fighting is not much worse than hugging," was a favourite saying of his, and once he had located Mr. J.G. Reeder, the night-hawk—and that had been the labour of months—the rest was easy. Always providing that Mr. Reeder was amenable to argument.

The middle-aged woman who opened the door to him gave him an unpromising reception.

"Mr. Reeder is engaged," she said, "and he doesn't want to see any visitors."

"Will you kindly tell him," said Emanuel with his most winning smile and a beam of benevolence behind his thick glasses, "that Mr. Legge from Devonshire would like to see him on a very particular matter of business?"

She closed the door in his face, and kept him so long waiting that he decided that even the magic of his name and its familiar association (he guessed) had not procured him an entry. But here he was mistaken. The door was opened for him, closed and bolted behind him, and he was led up a flight of stairs to the first floor.

The house was, to all appearance, well and comfortably furnished. The room into which he was ushered, if somewhat bare and official-looking, had an austerity of its own. Sitting behind a large writing-table, his back to the fire-place, was a man whom he judged to be between fifty and sixty. His face was thin, his expression sad. Almost on the end of his nose was clipped a pair of large, circular pince-nez. His hair was of that peculiar tint, red turning to grey, and his ears were large and prominent, seeming to go away from his head at right angles. All this Emanuel noted in a glance.

"Good morning, or good afternoon, Mr. Legge," said the man at the desk. He half rose and offered a cold and lifeless hand. "Sit down, will you?" he said wearily. "I don't as a rule receive visitors, but I seem to remember your name. Now where have I heard it?"

He dropped his chin to his breast and looked over his spectacles dolefully. Emanuel's expansive smile struck against the polished surface of his indifference and rebounded. He felt for the first time the waste of expansiveness.

"I had a little piece of information I thought I'd bring to you, Mr. Reeder," he said. "I suppose you know that I'm one of those unfortunate people who, through the treachery of others, have suffered imprisonment?"

"Yes, yes, of course," said Mr. Reeder in his weak voice, his chin still bent, his pale blue eyes fixed unwaveringly on the other. "Of course, I remember. You were the man who robbed the strong-room. Of course you were. Legge, Legge? I seem to remember the name too. Haven't you a son?"

"I have a son, the best boy in the world," said Emanuel fervently.

There was a telephone receiver at Mr. Reeder's right hand, and throughout the interview he was polishing the black stem with the cuff of his alpaca coat, a nervous little trick which first amused and then irritated the caller.

"He has never been in trouble, Mr. Legge? Ah, that's a blessing," he sighed. "So many young people get into trouble nowadays."

If there was one person whom Legge did not want to discuss it was his son. He got off the subject as well as he could.

"I understand, Mr. Reeder, that you're doing special work for the Government—in the police department?"

"Not in the police department," murmured the other. "No, no, certainly not—not in the police department. I scarcely know a policeman. I see them often in the streets, and very picturesque figures they are. Mostly young men in the vigour and prime of youth. What a wonderful thing is youth, Mr. Legge! I suppose you're very proud of your son?"

"He's a good boy," said Emanuel shortly, and Mr. Reeder sighed again.

"Children are a great expense," he said. "I often wonder whether I ought to be glad that I never married. What is your son by occupation, Mr. Legge?"

"An export agent," said Emanuel promptly.

"Dear, dear!" said the other, and shook his head.

Emanuel did not know whether he was impressed or only sympathising.

"Being in Dartmoor, naturally I met a number of bad characters," said the virtuous Emanuel; "men who did not appeal to me, since I was perfectly innocent and only got my stretch—lagging—imprisonment through a conspiracy on the part of a man I've done many a good turn to—"

"Ingratitude," interrupted Mr. Reeder, drawing in his breath. "What a terrible thing is ingratitude! How grateful your son must be that he has a father who looks after him, who has properly educated him and brought him up in the straight way, in spite of his own deplorable lapses!"

"Now, look here, Mr. Reeder." Emanuel thought it was time to get more definitely to business. "I'm a very plain man, and I'm going to speak plainly to you. It has come to my knowledge that the gentlemen you are acting for are under the impression that my boy's got to do with the printing of 'slush'—counterfeit notes. I was never more hurt in my life than when I heard this rumour. I said to myself: 'I'll go straight away to Mr. Reeder and discuss the matter with him. I know he's a man of the world, and he will understand my feelings as a father.' Some people, Mr. Reeder"—his elbows were on the table and he leant over and adopted a more confidential tone—"Some people get wrong impressions. Only the other day somebody was saying to me: 'That Mr. Reeder is broke. He's got three county court summonses for money owed—'"

"A temporary embarrassment," murmured Mr. Reeder. "One has those periods of financial—er—depression."

He was polishing the stem of the telephone more vigorously.

"I don't suppose you're very well paid? I'm taking a liberty in making that personal statement, but as a man of the world you'll understand. I know what it is to be poor. I've had some of the best society people in my office"— Emanuel invented the office on the spur of the moment—"the highest people in the land, and if they've said: 'Mr. Legge, can you oblige me with a thousand or a couple of thousand?' why, I've pulled it out, as it were, like this."

He put his hand in his pocket and withdrew it, holding a large roll of money fastened with a rubber band.

For a second Mr. J.G. Reeder allowed his attention to be distracted, and surveyed the pile of wealth with the same detached interest which he had given to Emanuel. Then, reaching out his hand cautiously, he took the note from the top, felt it, fingered it, rustled it, and looked quickly at the watermark.

"Genuine money," he said in a hushed voice, and handed the note back with apparent reluctance.

"If a man is broke," said Legge emphatically, "I don't care who he is or what he is, I say: 'Is a thousand or two thousand any good to you?'—"

"And is it?" asked Mr. Reeder.

"Is what?" said Emanuel, taken off his guard.

"Is it any good to him?"

"Well, of course it is," said Legge. "My point is this: a gentleman may be very hard pressed, and yet be the most solvent person in the world. If he can only get a couple of thousand just when he wants it—why, there's no scandal, no appearance in court which might injure him in his job—"

"How very true! How very, *very* true!" Mr. Reeder seemed profoundly touched. "I hope you pass on these wise and original statements to your dear son, Mr. Legge?" he said. "What a splendid thing it is that he has such a father!"

Emanuel cursed him under his breath.

"Two thousand pounds," mused Mr. Reeder. "Now, if you had said five thousand pounds—"

"I do say five thousand," said Emanuel eagerly. "I'm not going to spoil the ship for a ha'porth of tar."

"If you had said five thousand pounds," Mr. Reeder went on, "I should have known that three thousand was 'slush,' or shall we say phoney'—because you only drew two thousand from the City and Birmingham Bank this morning, all in hundred pound notes, series GI.19721 to 19740. Correct me if I'm wrong. Of course, you might have some other genuine money stowed away in your little hotel, Mr. Legge; or your dear boy may have given you another three thousand as a sort of wedding present—I forgot, though, a bridegroom doesn't give wedding presents, does he? He receives them. How foolish of me! Put away your money, Mr. Legge. This room is very draughty, and it might catch cold. Do you ever go to the Hilly Fields? It is a delightful spot. You must come to tea with me one Sunday, and we will go up and hear the band. It is a very inexpensive but satisfactory method of spending two hours. As to those judgment summonses"—he coughed, and rubbed his nose with his long forefinger—"those summonses were arranged in order to bring you here. I did *so* want to meet you, and I knew the bait of my impecuniosity would be almost irresistible."

Emanuel Legge sat, dumbfounded.

"Do you know a man named 'Golden'? Ah, he would be before your time. Have you ever heard of him? He was my predecessor. I don't think you met him. He had a great saying—set a 'brief' to catch a thief. We called a note a 'brief' in those days. Good afternoon, Mr. Legge. You will find your way down."

Legge rose, and with that the sad-faced man dropped his eyes and resumed the work he had been at when the visitor had interrupted him.

"I only want to say this, Mr. Reeder—" began Legge.

"Tell my housekeeper," pleaded Reeder weakly, and he did not look up. "She's frightfully interested in fairy stories—I think she must be getting towards her second childhood. Good afternoon, Mr. Legge."

CHAPTER 12

Emanuel Legge was half-way home before he could sort out his impressions He went back to the Bloomsbury Hotel where he was staying There was no message for him, and there had been no callers It was now seven o'clock He wondered whether Jeff had restrained his impatience Jeff must be told and warned Johnny Gray, dead or maimed in a hospital, had ceased to be a factor Peter Kane, for all his cunning and his vengefulness, might be dismissed as a source of danger It was Mr JG Reeder who filled his thoughts: the bored Civil Servant with a weak voice, who had such a surprising knowledge of things, and whose continuous pointed references to Jeffrey filled him with unquiet Jeffrey must clear out of the country, and must go while the going was good If he hadn't been such a fool, he would have moved that night Now, that was impossible

Peter had not arrived at the Charlton, or the men whom Legge had set to watch would have reported. If it had not been for the disturbing interview he had had with Reeder, he would have been more worried about Peter Kane; for when Peter delayed action, he was dangerous.

At eight o'clock that night, a small boy brought him a note to the hotel. It was addressed "E. Legge," and the envelope was grimy with much handling. Emanuel took the letter to his room and locked the door before he opened it. It was from a man who was very much on the inside of things, one of Jeff's shrewd but illiterate assistants, first lieutenant of the Big Printer, and a man to be implicitly trusted.

There were six closely written pages, ill-spelt and blotted. Emanuel read the letter a dozen times, and when he finished, there was panic in his heart.

"Johnny Gray got out of the tunnel all right, and he's going to squeak to Reeder," was the dramatic beginning, and there was a great deal more....

Emanuel knew a club in the West End of London, and his name was numbered amongst the members, even in the days when he had little opportunity of exercising his membership. It was a club rather unlike any other, and occupied the third and fourth floor of a building, the lower floors being in the possession of an Italian *restaurateur*. Normally, the proprietor of a fairly popular restaurant would not hire out his upper floors to so formidable a rival; but the proprietors of the club were also proprietors of the building, the restaurant keeper being merely a tenant.

It suited the membership of the Highlow Club to have their premises a little remote. It suited them better that no stairway led from the lower to the upper floors. Members of the club went down a narrow passage by the side of the restaurant entrance. From the end of the passage ran a small elevator, which carried them to the third floor. The County Council, in granting this concession, insisted upon a very complete fire escape system outside the building—a command which very well suited the members. Some there were who found it convenient to enter the premises by this latter method, and a window leading into the club was left unfastened day and night against such a contingency.

On the flat roof of the building was a small superstructure, which was never used by the club members; whilst another part of the building which also belonged exclusively to the Highlow, was the basement, to which the restaurant proprietor had no access—much to his annoyance, since it necessitated the building of a wine storage room in the limited space in the courtyard behind.

Stepping out of the elevator into a broad passage, well carpeted, its austere walls hung with etchings, Emanuel Legge was greeted respectfully by the liveried porter who sat behind a desk within sight of the lift. There was every reason why Emanuel should be respected at the Highlow, for he was, in truth, the proprietor of the club, and his son had exercised control of the place during many of the years his father had been in prison.

The porter, who was a big ex-prize fighter, expressly engaged for the purpose for which he was frequently required, hurried from his tiny perch to stand deferentially before his master.

"Anybody here?" asked Legge.

The man mentioned a few names.

"Let me see the engagement book," said the other, and the man produced from beneath the ledge of his desk a small, red book, and Emanuel turned the pages. The old man's hand ran down the list, and suddenly stopped.

"Oh, yes," he said softly, closing the book and handing it back.

"Are you expecting anybody, Mr. Legge?" asked the porter.

"No, I'm not expecting anybody… only I wondered…"

"Mr. Jeffrey got married today, I hear, sir? I'm sure all the staff wish him joy."

All the staff did not wish Mr. Jeffrey Legge joy, for neither he nor his father were greatly popular, even in the tolerant society of the Highlow, and moreover, strange as it may appear, very few people knew him by sight.

"That's very good of you, very good indeed," murmured Emanuel absently.

"Are you dining here, sir?"

"No, no, I'm not dining here. I just looked in, that is all."

He stepped back into the elevator, and the porter watched it drop with pleasure. It was half-past eight; the glow was dying in the sky, and the lights were beginning to twinkle in the streets, as Emanuel walked steadily toward Shaftesbury Avenue.

Providentially, he was at the corner of a side street when he saw Peter Kane. He was near enough to note that under his thin overcoat Peter was in evening dress. Slipping into the doorway, he watched the man pass. Peter was absorbed in thought; his eyes were on the ground, and he had no interest for anything but the tremendous problem which occupied his mind.

Legge came back to the corner of the street and watched him furtively. Opposite the club, Peter stopped, looked up for a while, and passed on. The watcher laughed to himself. That club could have no pleasant memories for Peter Kane that night; it was in the Highlow that he had met the "young Canadian officer" and had "rescued" him, as he had thought, from his dangerous surroundings. There had Peter been trapped, for the introduction of Jeff Legge was most skilfully arranged. Going into the club one night, Peter saw, as he thought, a young, good-looking soldier boy in the hands of a gang of cardsharpers, and the "rescued officer" had been most grateful, and had called upon Peter at the earliest opportunity. So simple, so very simple, to catch Peter. It would be a more difficult matter, thought Emanuel, for Peter to catch *him*.

He waited until the figure had disappeared in the gloom of the evening, and then walked back to the Avenue. This comedy over, there remained the knowledge of stark tragedy, of danger to his boy, and the upsetting of all his plans, and, the most dreadful of all possibilities, the snaring of the Big Printer. This night would the battle be fought, this night of nights would victory or defeat be in his hands. Reeder—Johnny—Peter Kane—all opposed him, innocent of their co-operation, and in his hands a hostage beyond price—the body and soul of Marney Legge.

He had scarcely disappeared when another person known to him came quickly along the quiet street, turned into the club entrance, and, despite the expostulations of the elevator man, insisted upon being taken up. The porter had heard the warning bell and stood waiting to receive her when the door of the elevator opened.

"Where's Emanuel?" she asked.

"Just gone," said the porter.

"That's a lie. I should have seen him if he'd just gone."

She was obviously labouring under some emotion, and the porter, an expert on all stages of feminine emotionalism, shrewdly diagnosed the reason for her wildness of manner and speech.

"Been a wedding today, hasn't there?" he asked with heavy jocularity. "Now, Lila, what's the good of kicking up a fuss? You know you oughtn't to come here. Mr. Legge gave orders you weren't to be admitted whilst you were at Kane's."

"Where is Emanuel?" she asked.

"I tell you he's just gone out," said the porter in a tone of ponderous despair. "What a woman you are! You don't believe anything!"

"Has he gone back to his hotel?"

"That's just where he has gone. Now be wise, girl, and beat it. Anybody might be coming here—Johnny Gray was in last night, and he's a pal of Peter's."

"Johnny knows all about me," she said impatiently. "Besides, I've left Peter's house."

She stood undecidedly at the entrance of the open elevator, and then, when the porter was preparing some of his finest arguments for her rapid disappearance, she stepped into the lift and was taken down.

The Highlow was a curious club, for it had no common room. Fourteen private dining-rooms and a large and elegantly furnished card-room constituted the premises. Meals were served from the restaurant below, being brought up by service lift to a small pantry. The members of the club had not the club feeling in the best sense of the word. They included men and women, but the chief reason for the club's existence was that it afforded a safe and not unpleasant meeting-place for members of the common class, and gave necessary seclusion for the slaughter of such innocents as came within the influence of its more dexterous members. How well its inner secrets were kept is best illustrated by the fact that Peter Kane had been a member for twenty years without knowing that his sometime companion in crime had any official connection with its control. Nor was it ever hinted to him that the man who was directing the club's activities during Emanuel's enforced absence, was his son.

Peter was a very infrequent visitor to the Highlow; and indeed, on the occasion of his first meeting with the spurious Major Floyd, he had been tricked into coming, though this he did not know.

The porter was busy until half-past nine. Little parties came, were checked off in the book, and then—he looked at his watch.

"Twenty-five to ten," he said, and pushed a bell button.

A waiter appeared from the side passage.

"Put a bottle of wine in No. 13," he said.

The waiter looked at him surprised.

"No. 13?" he said, as if he could not believe his ears.

"I said it," confirmed the porter.

* * * *

Jeffrey ate a solitary dinner. The humour of the situation did not appeal to him. On his honeymoon, he and his wife were dining, a locked door between them. But he could wait.

Again he tried the queer-shaped pliers upon the key of the second bedroom. The key turned readily. He put the tool into his pocket with a sense of power. The clatter of a table being cleared came to him from the other room, and presently he heard the outer door close and a click of the key turning. He lit his fourth cigar and stepped out on to the balcony, surveying the crowded street with a dispassionate interest. It was theatre time. Cars were rolling up to the Haymarket; the long queue that he had seen waiting at the doors of the cheaper parts of the house had disappeared; a restaurant immediately opposite was blazing with lights; and on a corner of the street a band of ex-soldiers were playing the overture of "Lohengrin."

Glancing down into the street, he distinguished one of the "minders" his father had put there for his protection, and grinned. Peter could not know; he would have been here before. As to Johnny...? Emanuel had been very confident that Johnny presented no danger, and it rather looked as though Emanuel's view was right. But if Peter knew, why hadn't he come?

He strolled back to the room, looked at the girl's door and walked toward it.

"Marney!" he called softly.

There was no answer. He knocked on the panel.

"Marney, come along. I want to talk to you. You needn't open the door. I just wanted to ask you something."

Still there was no answer. He tried the door: it was locked.

"Are you there?" he called sharply, but she did not reply.

He pulled the pliers from his pocket, and, pushing the narrow nose into the keyhole, gripped the end of the key and turned it. Then, flinging open the door, he rushed in.

The room was empty, and the big bathroom that led out of the suite was empty also. He ran to the passage door: it was locked—locked from the outside. In a sweat of fear he flew through the saloon into the corridor, and the first person he saw was the floor waiter.

"Madam, sir? Yes, she went out a little time ago."

"Went out, you fool? Where?" stormed Jeff.

"I don't know, sir. She just went out. I saw her going along the corridor."

Jeff seized his hat and went down the stairs three at a time. The reception clerk had not seen the girl, nor had any of the pages, or the porter on the door. Oblivious to any immediate danger, he dashed out into the street, and, looking up and down, saw the minder and called him.

"She hasn't come out this entrance. There's another in Pall Mall," he explained. "Jimmy Low's there."

But the second man on the Pall Mall entrance had not seen her either. Jeff went back to interview the manager.

"There is no other way out, sir, unless she went down the service stairs."

"It was that cursed maid, the Welsh woman," snarled Jeffrey. "Who is she? Can I see her?"

"She went off duty this afternoon, sir," said the manager. "Is there anything I can do? Perhaps the lady has gone out for a little walk? Does she know London?"

Jeff did not stop to reply: he fled up the stairs, back to the room, and made a quick search. The girl's dressing-case, which he knew had been taken into the bedroom, was gone. Something on the floor attracted his attention. He picked it up, and read the few scribbled lines, torn from a notebook; and as he read, a light came into his eyes. Very carefully he folded the crumpled sheet and put it into his pocket. Then he went back to his sitting-room, and sat for a long time in the big arm-chair, his legs thrust out before him, his hands deep in his trousers pockets, and his thoughts were not wholly unpleasant.

The light was now nearly gone, and he got up.

"Room thirteen," he said. "Room thirteen is going to hold a few surprises tonight!"

CHAPTER 13

To Parker, the valet, as he laid out Johnny's dress clothes, there was a misfortune and a tragedy deeper than any to which Johnny had been a spectator Johnny, loafing into his bedroom, a long, black, ebonite cigarette-holder between his teeth, found his man profoundly agitated

"The buckle of your white dress waistcoat has in some unaccountable way disappeared," he said in a hushed voice. "I'm extremely sorry, sir, because this is the only white dress waistcoat you have."

"Be cheerful," said Johnny. "Take a happier view of life. You can tie the tapes behind. You could even sew me together, Parker. Are you an expert needle-worker, or do you crochet?"

"My needlework has been admired, sir," said Parker complacently. "I think yours is an excellent suggestion. Otherwise, the waistcoat will not sit as it should. Especially in the case of a gentleman with your figure."

"Parker," said Johnny, as he began to dress leisurely, "have you ever killed a man?"

"No, sir, I have never killed a man," said Parker gravely. "When I was a young man, I once ran over a cat—I was a great cyclist in my youth."

"But you never killed a man? And, what is more, you've never even wanted to kill a man?"

"No, sir, I can't say that I ever have," said Parker after a few moments' consideration, as though it were possible that some experience had been his which had been overlooked in the hurry of his answering.

"It is quite a nice feeling, Parker. Is there a hip pocket to these—yes, there is," he said, patting his trousers.

"I'm sorry there is," said Parker, "very sorry indeed. Gentlemen get into the habit of carrying their cigarette cases in the hip pocket, with the result that the coat tail is thrown out of shape. That is where the dinner jacket has its advantages—the Tuxedo, as an American gentleman once called it, though I've never understood why a dinner jacket should be named after a Scottish town."

"Tuxedo is in Dixie," said Johnny humorously, "and Dixie is America's lost Atlantis. Don't worry about the set of my tail coat. I am not carrying my cigarette case there."

"Anything more bulky would of course be worse, sir," said Parker, and Johnny did not carry the discussion any farther.

"Get me a cab," he ordered.

When Parker returned, he found his master was fully dressed.

"You will want your cane, sir. Gentlemen are carrying them now in evening dress. There is one matter I would like to speak to you about before you go—it is something that has been rather worrying me for the past few days."

Johnny was leaving the room, and turned.

"Anything serious?" he asked, for a moment deceived.

"I don't like telling you, sir, but I have discussed the matter with very knowledgeable people, and they are agreed that French shapes are no longer worn in silk hats. You occasionally see them in theatrical circles—"

Johnny put up a solemn hand.

"Parker, do not let us discuss my general shabbiness. I didn't even know I had a hat of French shape." He took off his hat and looked at it critically. "It is a much better shape than the hat I was wearing a week ago, Parker, believe me!"

"Of course I believe you, sir," agreed Parker, and turned to the door.

Johnny dismissed his cab in Shaftesbury Avenue and walked down toward the club. It was dark now; half-past nine had chimed as he came along Piccadilly.

It was a point of honour with all members of the Highlow that nobody drove up to the club, and its very existence was unknown to the taximen. That was a rule that had been made, and most faithfully adhered to; and the members of the Highlow observed their rules, for, if a breach did not involve a demand for their resignation, it occasionally brought about a broken head.

Just before he reached the club, he saw somebody cross the road. It was not difficult to recognise Jeff Legge. Just at that moment it would have been rather embarrassing for Johnny to have met the man. He turned and walked back the way he had come, to avoid the chance of their both going up in the elevator together.

Jeff Legge was in a hurry: the elevator did not move fast enough for him, and he stepped out on to the third floor and asked a question.

"No, sir, nobody has come. If they do, I'll send them along to you. Where will you be? You haven't a room engaged—your own room is taken. We don't often let it, but we're full tonight, and Mr. Legge raised no objection."

"No, I don't object," said Jeff; "but don't you worry about that. Let me see the book."

Again the red-covered engagement book was opened. Jeff read and nodded.

"Fine," he said. "Now tell me again who is here."

"There is Mr. George Kurlu, with a party of friends in No. 3; there's Mr. Bob Albutt and those two young ladies he goes about with—they're in No. 4." And so he recited until he came to No. 13.

"I know all about No. 13," said Jeff Legge between his teeth. "You needn't bother about me, however. That will do."

He strode along the carpeted hallway, turned abruptly into the right-angled passage, and presently stopped before a door with a neat golden "13" painted on its polished panel. He opened the door and went in. On the red-covered table was a bottle of wine and two glasses.

It was a moderately large room, furnished with a sofa, four dining chairs and a deep easy chair, whilst against one wall was a small buffet. The room was brilliantly lighted. Six bracket lamps were blazing; the centre light above the table, with its frosted bulbs, was full on. He did not shut the door, leaving it slightly ajar. There was too much light for his purpose. He first switched out the bracket lamps, and then all but one of the frosted bulbs in the big shaded lamp over the table. Then he sat down, his back to the door, his eyes on the empty fire-grate.

Presently he heard a sound, the whining of the elevator, and smiled. Johnny stepped out to the porter's desk with a friendly nod.

"Good evening, Captain," said the porter with a broad grin. "Glad to see you back, sir. I wasn't here last night when you came in. Hope you haven't had too bad a time in the country?"

"Abroad, my dear fellow, abroad," murmured the other reproachfully, and the porter chuckled. "Same old crowd, I suppose?"

"Yes, sir."

"Same old bolt down the fire-escape when the busies' call—or have you got all the busies' straightened?"

"I don't think there's much trouble, sir," said the porter. "We often have a couple of those gentlemen in here to dinner. The club's very convenient sometimes. I shouldn't think they'll ever shut us up."

"I shouldn't think so, either," said Johnny. "Which of the busies' do you get?"

"Well, sir, we get Mr. Craig, and—once we had that Reeder. He came here alone, booked a table and came alone! Can you beat it? Came and had his dinner, saw nobody and went away again. I don't think he's right up there"—he tapped his forehead significantly. "Anything less like a busy' I've never seen."

"I don't know whether he is a detective," said Johnny carelessly. "From all I've heard, he has nothing whatever to do with the police."

"Private, is he?" said the other in a tone of disappointment.

"Not exactly private. Anyway," with a smile, "he's not going to bother you or our honourable members. Anybody here?"

The porter looked to left and right, and lowered his voice.

"A certain person you know is here," he said meaningly.

Johnny laughed.

"It would be a funny club if there wasn't somebody I knew," he said. "Don't worry about me; I'll find a little corner for myself...."

Jeff looked at his watch; it was a quarter to ten, and he glanced up at the light; catching a glimpse of himself in the mirror of the buffet, was satisfied.

Room 13! And Marney was his wife! The blood surged up into his face, gorging the thick veins in his temples at the thought. She should pay! He had helped the old man, as he would help him in any graft, but he had never identified himself so completely with the plan as he did at that moment.

"Put her down to the earth," had said Emanuel, and by God he would do it. As for Johnny Gray...

The door opened stealthily, and a hand came in, holding a Browning. He heard the creak of the door but did not look round, and then:

"*Bang!*"

Once the pistol fired. Jeff felt a sharp twitch of pain, exquisite, unbearable, and fell forward on his knees.

Twice he endeavoured to rise, then with a groan fell in a huddled heap, his head in the empty fire-place.

CHAPTER 14

The doors and the walls of the private dining-rooms were almost sound-proof No stir followed the shot In the hall outside, the porter lifted his head and listened

"What was that?" he asked the waiting elevator man.

"Didn't hear anything," said the other laconically. "Somebody slammed a door."

"Maybe," said the porter, and went back to his book. He was filling in the names of that night's visitors, an indispensable record in such a club, and he was filling them in with pencil, an equally necessary act of caution, for sometimes the club members desired a quick expungement of this evidence.

In Room 13 silence reigned. A thin blue cloud floated to the ceiling; the door opened a little farther, and Johnny Gray came in, his right hand in his overcoat pocket.

Slowly he crossed the room to where the huddled figure lay, and, stooping, turned it upon its back. Then, after a brief scrutiny, his quick hands went through the man's pockets. He found something, carried it to the light, read with a frown and pushed the paper into his own pocket. Going out, he closed the door carefully behind him and strolled back to the hall.

"Not staying, Captain?" asked the porter in surprise.

"No, nobody I know here. Queer how the membership changes."

The man on duty was too well trained to ask inconvenient questions.

"Excuse me, Captain." He went over to Johnny and bent down. "You've got some blood on your cuff."

He took out his handkerchief and wiped the stain clean. Then his frowning eyes met the young man's.

"Anything wrong, Captain?"

"Nothing that I can tell you about," said Johnny. "Good night."

"Good night, sir," said the porter.

He stood by his desk, looking hard at the glass doors of the elevator, heard the rattle of the gate as it opened, and the whine of the lift as it rose again.

"Just stay here, and don't answer any rings till I come back," he said.

He hurried along the corridor into the side passage and, coming to No. 13, knocked. There was no answer. He turned the handle. One glance told him all he wanted to know. Gently he closed the door and hurried back to the telephone on his desk.

Before he raised the receiver he called the gaping lift-boy.

"Go to all the rooms, and say a murder has been committed. Get everybody out."

He was still clasping the telephone with damp hands when the last frightened guest crowded into the elevator, then:

"Highlow Club speaking. Is that the Charing Cross Hospital?... I want an ambulance here... Yes, 38, Boburn Street... There's been an accident."

He rung off and called another number.

"Highlow Club. Is that the police station?... It's the porter at the Highlow Club speaking, sir. One of our members has shot himself."

He put down the instrument and turned his face to the scared elevator man who had returned to the high level. At the end of the passage stood a crowd of worried waiters.

"Benny," he said, "Captain Gray hasn't been here tonight. You understand? Captain—Gray—has—not—been—here—to-night."

The guest-book was open on the desk. He took his pencil and wrote, on the line where Johnny Gray's name should have been, "Mr. William Brown of Toronto."

CHAPTER 15

The last of the guests had escaped, when the police came, and, simultaneously with the ambulance, Divisional-Inspector Craig, who had happened to be making a call in the neighbourhood The doctor who came with the ambulance made a brief examination

"He is not dead, though he may be before he reaches hospital," he said.

"Is it a case of suicide?"

The doctor shook his head.

"Suicides do not, as a rule, shoot themselves under the right shoulder-blade. It would be a difficult operation: try it yourself. I should say he'd been shot from the open doorway."

He applied a rough first dressing, and Jeffrey was carried into the elevator. In the bottom passage a stretcher was prepared, and upon this he was laid, and, covered with a blanket, carried through the crowd which had assembled at the entrance.

"Murder, or attempted murder, as the case may be," said Craig. "Someone has tipped off the guests. You, I suppose, Stevens? Let me see your book."

The inspector ran his finger down the list, and stopped at Room 13.

"Mr. William Brown of Toronto. Who is Mr. Brown of Toronto?"

"I don't know, sir. He engaged a room by telephone. I didn't see him go."

"That old fire-escape of yours still working?" asked Craig sardonically. "Anybody else been here? Who is the wounded man? His face seemed familiar to me."

"Major Floyd, sir."

"Who?" asked Craig sharply. "Impossible! Major Floyd is—"

It *was* Floyd! He remembered now. Floyd, with whom he had sat that day—that happily-married man!

"What was he doing here?" he asked. "Now, spill it, Stevens, unless you want to get yourself into pretty bad trouble."

"I've spilled all I know, sir," said Stevens doggedly. "It was Major Floyd."

And then an inspiration came to him.

"If you want to know who it was, it was Jeff Legge. Floyd's his fancy name."

"Who?"

Craig had had many shocks in his life, but this was the greatest he had had for years.

"Jeff Legge? Old Legge's son?"

Stevens nodded.

"Nobody knows that but a couple of us," he said. "Jeff doesn't work in the light."

The officer nodded slowly.

"I've never seen him," he admitted. "I knew Legge had a son, but I didn't know he was running crook. I thought he was a bit of a boy."

"He's some boy, let me tell you!" said Stevens.

Craig sat down, his chin in his hands.

"Mrs. Floyd will have to be told. Good God! Peter Kane's daughter! Peter didn't know that he'd married her to Legge's son?"

"I don't know whether he knew or not," said Stevens, "but if I know old Peter, he'd as soon know that she'd gone to the devil as marry her to a son of Emanuel Legge's. I'm squeaking in a way," he said apologetically, "but you've got to know—Emanuel will tell you as soon as he gets the news."

"Come here," said Craig. He took the man's arm and led him to the passage where the detectives were listening, opened the door of a private room, the table giving evidence of the hasty flight of the diners. "Now," he said, closing the door, "what's the strength of this story?"

"I don't know it all, Mr. Craig, but I know they were putting a point on Peter Kane a long time ago. Then one night they brought Peter along and kidded him into thinking that Jeff was a sucker in the hands of the boys. Peter had never seen Jeff before—as a matter of fact, *I* didn't know he was Jeff at the time; I'd heard a lot about him, but, like a lot of other people, I hadn't seen him. Well, they fooled Peter all right. He took the lad away with him. Jeff was wearing a Canadian officer's uniform, and, of course, Jeff told the tale. He wouldn't be the son of his father if he didn't. That's how he got to know the Kanes, and was taken to their home. When I heard about the marriage, I thought Peter must have known. I never dreamt they were playing a trick on him."

"Peter didn't know," said Craig slowly. "Where's the girl?"

"I can't tell you. She's in London somewhere."

"At the Charlton," nodded the other. "Now, you've got to tell me, Stevens, who is Mr. Brown of Toronto? It's written differently from your usual hand—written by a man who has had a bad scare. In other words, it was written after you'd found the body."

Stevens said nothing.

"You saw him come out: who was he?"

"If I die this minute—" began Stevens.

"You might in a few months, as 'accessory after,'" said the other ominously; "and that's what you'll do if you conceal a murderer. Who is Mr. Brown?"

Stevens was struggling with himself, and after a while it came out.

"Johnny was here tonight," he said huskily. "Johnny Gray."

Craig whistled.

There was a knock at the door. A police officer, wanting instructions.

"There's a woman down below, pretty nigh mad. I think you know her, sir."

"Not Lila?" blurted Stevens.

"That's the girl. Shall I let her come up?"

"Yes," said Craig. "Bring her in here."

She came in a minute, distracted, incoherent, her hair dishevelled, her hands trembling.

"Is he dead?" she gasped. "For God's sake tell me. I see it in your face—he's dead. Oh, Jeff, Jeff!"

"Now you sit down," said the kindly Craig. "He's no more dead than you or I are. Ask Stevens. Jeff's doing very well indeed. Just a slight wound, my dear—nothing to worry about. What was the trouble? Do you know anything about it?"

She could not answer him.

"He's dead," she moaned. "My God, I killed him! I saw him and followed him here!"

"Give her a glass of wine, Stevens."

The porter poured out a glass of white wine from one of the many deserted bottles on the table, and put it to her chattering teeth.

"Now, Lila, let's get some sense out of you. I tell you, Jeff's not dead. What is he to you, anyway?"

"Everything," she muttered. She was shivering from head to foot. "I married him three years ago. No, I didn't," she said in a sudden frenzy.

"Go on; tell us the truth," said Craig. "We're not going to pull him for bigamy, anyway."

"I married him three years ago," she said. "He wasn't a bad fellow to me. It was the old man's idea, his marrying this girl, and there was a thousand for me in it. He put me down in Horsham to look after her, and see that there were no letters going to Johnny. There wasn't any need of that, because she never wrote. I didn't like the marriage idea, but he swore to me that it was only to get Peter's money, and I believed him. Then tonight he told me the truth, knowing I wouldn't squeak. I wish to God I had now, I wish I had! He is dead, isn't he? I know he's dead!"

"He's not dead, you poor fish," said Craig impatiently. "I might be congratulating you if he was. No, he's got a bit of a wound."

"Who shot him?"

"That's just what I want to know," said Craig. "Was it you?"

"Me!" Her look of horror supplied a satisfactory answer to his question. "No, I didn't. I didn't know he was here, or coming here. I thought he was at the hotel, till I saw him. Yet I had a feeling that he was coming here tonight, and I've been waiting about all evening. I saw Peter and dodged him."

"Peter? Has he been near the club?"

She shook her head.

"I don't know. He was on his way. I thought he was going to the Highlow. There's nowhere else he'd go in this street—I saw him twice."

Craig turned his bright, suspicious eyes upon the porter.

"Peter been here? I didn't see anything about Mr. Brown of Montreal?" he asked sarcastically.

"No, he hasn't. I haven't seen Peter since the Lord knows when," said the porter emphatically. "That's the truth. You can give the elevator boy permission to tell you all he knows, and if Peter was here tonight you can hang me."

Craig considered for a long time.

"Does Peter know his way in by the easy route?" he asked.

"You mean the fire-escape? Yes, Peter knows that way, but members never come in by the back nowadays. They've got nothing to hide."

Craig went out of the room and walked down the passage, stopping at No. 13. Immediately opposite the door was a window, and it was wide open. Beyond was the grille of the fire-escape landing. He stepped out through the window and peered down into the dark yard where the escape ended. By the light of a street lamp he saw a stout gate, in turn pierced by a door, and this led to the street. The door was open, a fact which might be accounted for by the presence in the yard of two uniformed policemen, the flash of whose lanterns he saw. He came back into the corridor and to Stevens.

"Somebody may have used the fire-escape tonight, and they may not," he said. "What time did Gray come in? Who came in first?"

"Jeff came first, about five minutes before Gray."

"Then what happened?"

"I had a chat with Captain Gray," said the porter, after a second's hesitation. "He went round into the side passage—"

"The same way that Jeff had gone?"

The porter nodded.

"About a minute later—in fact, it was shorter than a minute—I heard what I thought was a door slammed. I remarked upon the fact to the elevator man."

"And then?"

"I suppose four or five minutes passed after that, and Captain Gray came out. Said he might look in later."

"There was no sign of a struggle in Captain Gray's clothes?"

"No, sir. I'm sure there was no struggle."

"I should think not," agreed Craig. "Jeff Legge never had a chance of showing fight."

The girl was lying on the sofa, her head buried in her arms, her shoulders shaking, and the sound of her weeping drew the detective's attention to her.

"Has she been here before tonight?"

"Yes, she came, and I had to throw her out—Emanuel told me she was not to be admitted."

Craig made a few notes in his book, closed it with a snap and put it in his pocket.

"You understand, Stevens, that, if you're not under arrest, you're under open arrest. You'll close the club for tonight and admit no more people. I shall leave a couple of men on the premises."

"I'll lock up the beer," said Stevens facetiously.

"And you needn't be funny," was the sharp retort. "If we close this club you'll lose your job—and if they don't close it now they never will."

He took aside his assistant.

"I'm afraid Johnny's got to go through the hoop tonight," he said. "Send a couple of men to pull him in. He lives at Albert Mansions. I'll go along and break the news to the girl, and somebody'll have to tell Peter—I hope there's need for Peter to be told," he added grimly.

CHAPTER 16

A surprise awaited him when he came to the Charlton Mrs Floyd had gone—
nobody knew whither Her husband had followed her some time afterwards,
and neither had returned Somebody had called her on the telephone, but had
left no name

"I know all about her husband not returning," said Craig. "But haven't
you the slightest idea where the lady is?"

The negative reply was uncompromising.

"Her father hasn't been here?"

His informant hesitated.

"Yes, sir; he was on Mrs. Floyd's floor when she was missing—in fact,
when Major Floyd was down here making inquiries. The floor waiter recognised him, but did not see him come or go."

Calling up the house at Horsham he learnt, what he already knew, that
Peter was away from home. Barney, who answered him, had heard nothing
of the girl; indeed, this was the first intimation he had had that all was not
well. And a further disappointment lay in store for him. The detective he had
sent to find Johnny returned with the news that the quarry had gone. Accord-
ing to the valet, his master had returned and changed in a hurry, and, taking
a small suitcase, had gone off to an unknown destination.

An inquiry late that night elicited the fact that Jeff was still living, but
unconscious. The bullet had been extracted, and a hopeful view was taken of
the future. His father had arrived early in the evening, and was half mad with
anxiety and rage.

"And if he isn't quite mad by the morning, I shall be surprised," said the
surgeon. "I'm going to keep him here and give him a little bromide to ease
him down."

"Poison him," suggested Craig.

When the old detective was on the point of going home, there arrived a
telephone message from the Horsham police, whom he had enlisted to watch
Peter's house.

"Mr. Kane and his daughter arrived in separate motorcars at a quarter
past twelve," was the report. "They came within a few minutes of one another."

Craig was on the point of getting through to the house, but thought better of it. A fast police car got him to Horsham under the hour, the road being

clear and the night a bright one. Lights were burning in Peter's snuggery, and it was he himself who, at the sound of the motor wheels, came to the door.

"Who's that?" he asked, as Craig came up the dark drive, and, at the sound of the detective's voice, he came half-way down the drive to meet him. "What's wrong, Craig? Anything special?"

"Jeff's shot. I suppose you know who Jeff is?"

"I know, to my sorrow," said Peter Kane promptly. "Shot? How? Where?"

"He was shot this evening between a quarter to ten and ten o'clock, at the Highlow Club."

"Come in. You'd better not tell my girl—she's had as much as she can bear tonight. Not that I'm worrying a damn about Jeff Legge. He'd better die, and die quick, for if I get him—"

He did not finish his sentence, and the detective drew the man's arm through his.

"Now, listen, Peter, you've got to go very slow on this case, and not talk such a darned lot. You're under suspicion too, old man. You were seen in the vicinity of the club."

"Yes, I was seen in the vicinity of the club," repeated Peter, nodding. "I was waiting there—well, I was waiting there for a purpose. I went to the Charlton, but my girl had gone—I suppose they told you—and then I went on to the Highlow, and saw that infernal Lila—by the way, she's one of Jeff's women, isn't she?"

"To be exact," said the other quietly, "she's his wife."

Peter Kane stopped dead.

"His wife?" he whispered. "Thank God for that! Thank God for that! I forgive her everything. Though she is a brute—how a woman could allow—but I can't judge her. That graft has always been dirty to me. It is hateful and loathsome. But, thank God she's his wife, Craig!" Then: "Who shot this fellow?"

"I don't know. I'm going to pull Johnny for it."

They were in the hall, and Peter Kane spun round, open-mouthed, terror in his eyes.

"You're going to pull Johnny?" he said. "Do you know what you're saying, Craig? You're mad! Johnny didn't do it. Johnny was nowhere near—"

"Johnny was there. And, what is more, Johnny was in the room, either at the moment of the shooting or immediately after. The elevator boy has spoken what's in his mind, which isn't much, but enough to convict Johnny if this fellow dies."

"Johnny there!" Peter's voice did not rise above a whisper.

"I tell you frankly, Peter, I thought it was you."

Craig was facing him squarely, his keen eyes searching the man's pallid face. "When I heard you were around, and that you had got to know that this fellow was a fake. Why were you waiting?"

"I can't tell you that—not now," said the other, after turning the matter over in his mind. "I should have seen Johnny if he was there. I saw this girl, Lila, and I was afraid she'd recognise me. I think she did, too. I went straight on into Shaftesbury Avenue, to a bar I know. I was feeling queer over this—this discovery of mine. I can prove I was there from a quarter to ten till ten, if you want any proof. Oh, Johnny, Johnny!"

All this went on in the hall. Then came a quick patter of footsteps, and Marney appeared in the doorway.

"Who is it—Johnny? Oh, it is you, Mr. Craig? Has anything happened?" She looked in alarm from face to face. "Nothing has happened to Johnny?"

"No, nothing has happened to Johnny," said Craig soothingly. He glanced at Peter. "You ought to know this, Marney," he said. "I can call you Marney—I've known you since you were five. Jeff Legge has been shot."

He thought she was going to faint, and sprang to catch her, but with an effort of will she recovered.

"Jeff shot?" she asked shakily. "Who shot him?"

"I don't know. That's just what we are trying to discover. Perhaps you can help us. Why did you leave the hotel. Was Johnny with you?"

She shook her head.

"I haven't seen Johnny," she said, "but I owe him—everything. There was a woman in the hotel." She glanced timidly at her father. "I think she was an hotel thief or something of the sort. She was there to—to steal. A big Welsh woman."

"A Welshwoman?" said Craig quickly. "What is her name?"

"Mrs. Gwenda Jones. Johnny knew about her, and telephoned her to tell her to take care of me until he could get to me. She got me out of the hotel, and then we walked down the Duke of York steps into the Mall. And then a curious thing happened—I was just telling daddy when you came. Mrs. Jones—she's such a big woman—"

"I know the lady," said Craig.

"Well, she disappeared. She wasn't exactly swallowed up by the earth," she said with a faint smile, "and she didn't go without warning. Suddenly she said to me: 'I must leave you now, my dear. I don't want that man to see me.' I looked round to find who it was that she was so terribly afraid of, and there seemed to be the most harmless lot of people about. When I turned, Mrs. Jones was running up the steps. I didn't wish to call her back, I felt so ridiculous. And then a man came up to me, a middle-aged man with the saddest face you could imagine. I told you that, daddy?"

He nodded.

"He took his hat off—his hair was almost white—and asked me if my name was Kane. I didn't tell him the other name," she said with a shiver. "'May I take you to a place of safety, Miss Kane?' he said. 'I don't think you ought to be seen with that raw-boned female.' I didn't know what to do, I was so frightened, and I was glad of the company and protection of any man, and, when he called a cab, I got in without the slightest hesitation. He was such a gentle soul, Mr. Craig. He talked of nothing but the weather and chickens! I think we talked about chickens all the way to Lewisham."

"Are you sure it was Lewisham?"

"It was somewhere in that neighbourhood. What other places are there there?"

"New Cross, Brockley—" began Craig.

"That's the place—Brockley. It was the Brockley Road. I saw it printed on the corner of the street. He took me into his house. There was a nice, motherly old woman whom he introduced to me as his housekeeper."

"And what did he talk about?" asked the fascinated Craig.

"Chickens," she said solemnly. "Do you know what chickens lay the best eggs? I'm sure you don't. Do you know the best breed for England and the best for America? Do you know the most economical chickens to keep? I do! I wondered what he was going to do with me. I tried to ask him, but he invariably turned me back to the question of incubators and patent feeds, and the cubic space that a sitting hen requires as compared with an ordinary hen. It was the quaintest, most fantastic experience. It seems now almost like one of Alice's dreams! Then, at ten o'clock, I found a motorcar had come for me. 'I'm sending you home, young lady,' he said."

"Were you with him all the time, by the way?" asked Craig.

She shook her head.

"No, some part of the time I was with his housekeeper, who didn't even talk about chickens, but knitted large and shapeless jumpers, and sniffed. That was when he was telephoning; I knew he was telephoning because I could hear the drone of his voice."

"He didn't bring you back?"

"No, he just put me into the car and told me that I should be perfectly safe. I arrived just a few minutes ahead of daddy."

The detective scratched his chin, irritated and baffled.

"That's certainly got me," he said. "The raw-boned lady I know, but the chicken gentleman is mysterious. You didn't hear his name, by any chance?"

She shook her head.

"Do you know the number of the house?"

"Yes," she said frankly, "but he particularly asked me to forget it, and I've forgotten it." Then, in a more serious tone: "Is my—my—"

"Your nothing," interrupted Peter. "The blackguard was married—married to Lila. I think I must have gone daft, but I didn't realise this woman was planted in my house for a purpose. That type of girl wouldn't come at the wages if she had been genuine. Barney was always suspicious of her, by the way."

"Have you seen Johnny?" the girl asked Craig.

"No, I haven't seen him," said Craig carefully. "I thought of calling on him pretty soon."

Then it came to her in a flash, and she gasped.

"You don't think Johnny shot this man? You can't think that?"

"Of course he didn't shoot him," said Peter loudly. "It is a ridiculous idea. But you'll understand that Mr. Craig has to make inquiries in all sorts of unlikely quarters. You haven't been able to get hold of Johnny tonight?"

A glance passed between them, and Peter groaned.

"What a fool! What a fool!" he said. "Oh, my God, what a fool!"

"Father, Johnny hasn't done this? It isn't true, Mr. Craig. Johnny wouldn't shoot a man. Did anybody see him? How was he shot?"

"He was shot in the back."

"Then it wasn't Johnny," she said. "He couldn't shoot a man in the back!"

"I think, young lady," said Craig with a little smile, "that you'd better go to bed and dream about butterflies. You've had a perfect hell of a day, if you'll excuse my language. Say the firm word to her, Peter. Who's that?" He turned his head, listening.

"Barney," said Peter. "He has a distressing habit of wearing slippers. You can hear him miles away. He's opening the door to somebody—one of your people, perhaps. Or he's taking your chauffeur a drink. Barney has an enormous admiration for chauffeurs. They represent mechanical genius to him."

The girl was calmer now.

"I have too much to thank God for today, for this terrible thing to be true," she said in a low voice. "Mr. Craig, there is a mistake, I'm sure. Johnny couldn't have committed such a crime. It was somebody else—one of Jeffrey Legge's associates, somebody who hated him. He told me once that lots of people hated him, and I thought he was joking; he seemed so nice, so considerate. Daddy, I was mad to go through that, even to make you happy."

Peter Kane nodded.

"If you were mad, I was criminal, girlie," he said. "There was only one man in the world for you—"

The door opened slowly, and Barney sidled in.

"Johnny to see you folks," he said, and pulled the door wider.

John Gray was standing in the passage, and his eyes fell upon Craig with a look of quiet amusement.

CHAPTER 17

In another second the girl was in his arms, clinging to him, weeping convulsively on his shoulder, her face against his, her clasped hands about his neck

Craig could only look, wondering and fearing. Johnny would not have walked into the net unwarned. Barney would have told him that he was there. What amazed Craig, as the fact slowly dawned upon him, was that Johnny was still in evening dress. He took a step toward him, and gently Johnny disengaged the girl from his arms.

"I'd like to see the right cuff of your shirt, Johnny," said Craig.

Without a word, Gray held up his arm, and the inspector scrutinised the spotless linen, for spotless it was. No sign of a stain was visible.

"Either somebody's doing some tall lying, or you're being extraordinarily clever, Johnny. I'll see that other cuff if I may."

The second scrutiny produced no tangible result.

"Didn't you go home and change tonight?"

"No, I haven't been near my flat," he said.

Craig was staggered.

"But your man said that you came in, changed, took a suitcase and went away."

"Then Parker has been drinking," was the calm reply. "I have been enjoying the unusual experience of dining with the detective officer who was responsible for my holiday in Devonshire."

Craig took a step back.

"With Inspector Flaherty?" he asked.

Johnny nodded.

"With the good Inspector Flaherty. We have been exchanging confidences about our mutual acquaintances."

"But who was it went to your flat?" asked the bewildered Craig.

"My double. I've always contended that I have a double," said Johnny serenely.

He stood in the centre of the astounded group. Into Marney's heart had crept a wild hope.

"Johnny," she said, "was it this man who committed the crime for which you were punished?"

To her disappointment he shook his head.

"No, I am the gentleman who was arrested and sent to Dartmoor—my double stops short of these unpleasant experiences, and I can't say that I blame him."

"But do you mean to say that he deceived your servant?"

"Apparently," said Johnny, turning again to the detective who had asked the question.

"I take your word, of course, Johnny, as an individual."

Johnny chuckled.

"I like the pretty distinction. As an official, you want corroboration. Very well, that is not hard to get. If you take me back to Flaherty, he will support all I have told you."

Peter and the detective had the good taste to allow him to take leave of the girl without the embarrassment of their presence.

"It beats me—utterly beats me. Have you ever heard of this before, Peter?"

"That Johnny had a double? No, I can't say that I have."

"He may have invented the story for the sake of the girl. But there is the fact: he's in evening dress, whilst his servant distinctly described him as wearing a grey tweed suit. There is no mark of blood on his cuff, and I'm perfectly certain that Stevens wouldn't have tried to get Johnny in bad. He is very fond of the boy. Of course, he may be spinning this yarn for the sake of Marney, but it'll be easy enough to corroborate. I'll use your phone, Peter," he said suddenly. "I've got Flaherty's number in my book."

The biggest surprise of the evening came when a sleepy voice, undeniably Flaherty's, answered him.

"Craig's speaking. Who have you been dining with tonight, Flaherty?"

"You don't mean to tell me that you've called me up in the middle of the night," began the annoyed Irishman, "to ask me who I've been dining with?"

"This is serious, Flaherty. I want to know."

"Why, with Johnny, of course—Johnny Gray. I asked him to come to dinner."

"What time did he leave you?"

"Nearer eleven than ten," was the reply. "No, it was after eleven."

"And he was with you all that time? He didn't leave for a quarter of an hour?"

"Not for a quarter of a minute. We just talked and talked...."

Craig hung up the receiver and turned away from the instrument, shaking his head.

"Any other alibi would have hanged you, Johnny. But Flaherty's the straightest man in the C.I.D."

In view of what followed when Johnny reached his flat in the early hours of the morning, this testimony to the integrity of Inspector Flaherty seemed a little misguided.

"Nobody else been here?"

"No, sir," said Parker.

"What did you do with the shirt I took off?"

"I cut off the cuffs and burnt them, sir. I did it with a greater pleasure, because the rounded corner cuff is just a little *démodé*, if you do not mind my saying so, just a little—how shall I call it?—theatrical."

"The rest of the shirt—?"

"The rest of the shirt, sir," said Parker deferentially, "I am wearing. It is rather warm to wear two shirts, but I could think of no other way of disposing of it, sir. Shall I put your bath ready?"

Johnny nodded.

"If you will forgive the impertinence, did you succeed in persuading the gentleman you were going to see, to support your statement?"

"Flaherty? Oh, yes. Flaherty owes me a lot. Good night, Parker."

"Good night, sir. I hope you sleep well. Er—may I take that pistol out of your pocket, sir? It is spoiling the set of your trousers. Thank you very much."

He took the Browning gingerly between his finger and thumb and laid it on Johnny's writing-table.

"You don't mind my being up a little late, sir?" he said. "I think I would like to clean this weapon before I retire."

CHAPTER 18

Jeff Legge reclined in a long cane chair on a lawn which stretched to the edge of a cliff. Before him were the blue waters of the Channel, and the more gorgeous blue of an unflecked sky. He reached out his hand and took a glass that stood on the table by his side, sipped it with a wry face and called a name pettishly.

It was Lila who came running to his side.

"Take this stuff away, and bring me a whisky-and-soda," he said.

"The doctor said you weren't to have anything but lime juice. Oh, Jeff, you must do as he tells you," she pleaded.

"I'll break your head for you when I get up," he snarled. "Do as you're told. Where's the governor?"

"He's gone into the village to post some letters."

He ruminated on this, and then:

"If that busy comes, you can tell him I'm too ill to be seen."

"Who—Craig?"

"Yes," he growled, "the dirty, twisting thief! Johnny would have been in boob for this if he hadn't straightened Craig. If he didn't drop a thousand to keep off the moor, I'm a dead man!"

She pulled up a low chair to his side.

"I don't think Johnny did it," she said. "The old man thinks it was Peter. The window was found open after. He could have come in by the fire-escape—he knows the way."

He grumbled something under his breath, and very discreetly she did not press home her view.

"Where's Marney—back with her father?"

She nodded.

"Who told him I was married to you?"

"I don't know, Jeff," she said.

"You liar! You told him; nobody else could have known. If I get 'bird' for this marriage, I'll kill you, Lila. That's twice you've squeaked on me."

"I didn't know what I was saying. I was half mad with worry."

"I wish you'd gone the whole journey," he said bitterly. "It isn't the woman—I don't care a darn about that. It's the old man's quarrel, and he's got to get through with it. It's the other business being disorganised that's worrying me. Unless it's running like clockwork, you'll get a jam; and when you've got a jam, you collect a bigger crowd than I want to see looking at my operations. You didn't squeak about that, I suppose?"

"No, Jeff, I didn't know."

"And that's the reason you didn't squeak, eh?"

He regarded her unfavourably. And now she turned on him.

"Listen, Jeff Legge. I'm a patient woman, up to a point, and I'll stand for all your bad temper whilst you're ill. But you're living in a new age, Jeff, and you'd better wake up to the fact. All that Bill Sikes and Nancy stuff never did impress me. I'm no clinger. If you got really rough with me, I'd bat you, and that's a fact. It may not be womanly, but it's wise. I never did believe in the equality of the sexes, but no girl is the weaker vessel if she gets first grip of the kitchen poker."

Very wisely he changed the subject.

"I suppose they searched the club from top to bottom?" he said.

"They did."

"Did they look in the loft?"

"I believe they did. Stevens told me that they turned everything inside out."

He grunted.

"They're clever," he said. "It must be wonderful to be clever. Who's this?" He scowled across the lawn at a strange figure that had appeared, apparently by way of the cliff gate.

She rose and walked to meet the stooping stranger, who stood, hat in hand, waiting for her and smiling awkwardly.

"I'm so sorry to intrude," he said. "This is a beautiful place, is it not? If I remember rightly, this is the Dellsea Vicarage? I used to know the vicar—a very charming man. I suppose you have taken the house from him?"

She was half amused, half annoyed.

"This is Dellsea Vicarage," she said curtly. "Do you want to see anybody?"

"I wanted to see Mr. Jeffrey"—he screwed up his eyes and stared at the sky, as though trying to withdraw from some obscure cell of memory a name that would not come without special effort—"Mr. Jeffrey Legge—that is the name—Mr. Jeffrey Legge."

"He is very ill and can't be seen."

"I'm sorry to hear that," said the stranger, his mild face expressing the intensest sympathy. "Very sorry indeed."

He fixed his big, round glasses on the tip of his nose, for effect apparently, because he looked over them at her.

"I wonder if he would see me for just a few minutes. I've called to inquire about his health."

"What is your name?" she asked.

"Reeder—J.G. Reeder."

The girl felt her colour go, and turned quickly.

"I will ask him," she said.

Jeff heard the name and pursed his lips.

"That's the man the bank are running—or maybe it's the Government—to trail me," he said in a low tone. "Slip him along, Lila."

Mr. Reeder was beckoned across the lawn, and came with quick, mincing steps.

"I'm so sorry to see that you're in such a deplorable condition, Mr. Legge," he said. "I hope your father is well?"

"Oh, you've met the old man, have you?" said Jeffrey in surprise.

Mr. Reeder nodded.

"Yes; I have met your father," he said. "A very entertaining and a very ingenious man. Very!" The last word was spoken with emphasis.

Jeff was silent at this tribute to his parent's amiability.

"There has been a lot of talk in town lately about a certain nefarious business that is being carried on—surreptitiously, of course," said Mr. Reeder, choosing his words with care. "I, who live out of the world, and in the backwater of life, hear strange rumours about the distribution of illicit money—I think the cant term is 'slush' or 'slosh'—probably it is 'slush.'"

"It is 'slush,'" agreed Jeff, not knowing whether to be amused or alarmed, and watching the man all the time.

"Now I feel sure that the persons who are engaged in this practice cannot be aware of the enormously serious nature of their offence," said Mr. Reeder confidentially.

He broke off his lecture to look around the lawn and well-stocked garden that flanked it on either side.

"How beautiful is the world, Mr. Jeff—I beg your pardon, Mr. Legge," he said. "How lovely those flowers are! I confess that the sight of bluebells always brings a lump to my throat. I don't suppose they are bluebells," he added, "for it is rather late in the year. But that peculiar shade of blue. And those wonderful roses—I can smell them from here."

He closed his eyes, raised his nose and sniffed loudly—a ludicrous figure; but Jeff Legge did not laugh.

"I know very little, but I understand that in Dartmoor Prison there are only a few potted flowers, and that those are never seen by the prisoners, except by one privileged man whose task it is to tend them. A lifer, generally. Life without flowers must be very drab, Mr. Legge."

"I'm not especially fond of flowers," said Jeffrey.

"What a pity!" said the other regretfully. "What a thousand pities! But there is no sea view from that establishment, no painted ships upon a painted ocean—which is a quotation from a well-known poem; no delightful sense of freedom; nothing really that makes life durable for a man under sentence, let us say, of fifteen or twenty years."

Jeff did not reply.

"Do you love rabbits?" was the surprising question that was put to him.

"No, I can't say that I do."

Lila sat erect, motionless, all her senses trained to hear and understand.

Mr. Reeder sighed.

"I am very fond of rabbits. Whenever I see a rabbit in a cage or in a hutch, I buy it, take it to the nearest wood and release it. It may be a foolish kindness, because, born and reared in captivity, it may not have the necessary qualities to support itself amongst its wilder fellows. But I like letting rabbits loose; other people like putting rabbits in cages." He shook his finger in Jeffrey's face. "Never be a rabbit in a cage, Mr. Jeffrey—or is it Mr. Legge? Yes, Mr. Legge."

"I am neither a rabbit, nor a chicken, nor a fox, nor a skylark," said Jeffrey. "The cage hasn't been built that could hold me."

Again Mr. Reeder sighed.

"I remember another gentleman saying that some years ago. I forget in what prison he was hanged. Possibly it was Wandsworth—yes, I am sure it was Wandsworth. I saw his grave the other day. Just his initials. What a pity! What a sad end to a promising career! He is better off, I think, for twenty long years in a prison cell, that is a dreadful fate, Mr. Legge! And it is a fate that would never overtake a man who decided to reform. Suppose, let us say, he was forging Bank of England notes, and decided that he would burn his paper and his water-markers, dismiss all his agents... I don't think we should worry very much about that type of person. We should meet him generously and liberally, especially if his notes were of such excellent quality that they were difficult for the uninitiated to detect."

"What has happened to Golden?" asked Jeffrey boldly.

The eyes of the elderly man twinkled.

"Golden was my predecessor," he said. "A very charming fellow, by some accounts—"

Again Jeffrey cut him short.

"He used to be the man who was looking after the 'slush' for the police. Is he dead?"

"He has gone abroad," said Mr. Reeder gravely. "Yes, Mr. Golden could not stand this climate. He suffered terribly from asthma, or it may have been sciatica. I know there was an 'a' at the end of it. Did you ever meet him? Ah! You missed a very great opportunity," said Mr. Reeder. "Golden was a nice fellow—not as smart, perhaps, as he might have been, or as he should have been, but a very nice fellow. He did not work, perhaps, so much in the open as I do; and there I think he was mistaken. It is always an error to shut yourself up in an office and envelop yourself in an atmosphere of mystery. I myself am prone to the same fault. Now, my dear Mr. Legge, I am sure you will take my parable kindly, and will give it every thought and consideration."

"I would, if I were a printer of 'slush,' but, unfortunately, I'm not," said Jeffrey Legge with a smile.

"You're not, of course," the other hastened to say. "I wouldn't dream of suggesting you were. But with your vast circle of acquaintances—and, I'm sure, admirers—you may perhaps be able to convey my simple little illustration. I don't like to see rabbits in cages, or birds in cages, or anything else behind bars. And I think that Dartmoor is so—what shall I say?—unæsthetic. And it seems *such* a pity to spend all the years in Devonshire. In the spring, of course, it is delightful; in the summer it is hot; in the winter, unless you're at Torquay, it is deplorable. Good morning, Mr. Legge."

He bowed low to the girl, and, bowing, his spectacles fell off. Stooping, he picked them up with an apology and backed away, and they watched him in silence till he had disappeared from view.

CHAPTER 19

"What do you think of him for a busy?" asked Jeffrey contemptuously

She did not answer. Contact with the man had frightened her. It was not like Lila to shiver in the presence of detectives.

"I don't know what he is," she said a little breathlessly. "He's something like a... good-natured snake. Didn't you feel that, Jeffrey?"

"Good-natured nothing," said the other with a curl of his lip. "He's worse than Golden. These big corporations fall for that kind of man. They never give a chance to a real clever busy."

"Who was Golden?" she asked.

"He was an old fellow too. They fired him." He chuckled to himself. "And I was responsible for firing him. Then they brought in Mr. J.G. Reeder with a flourish of trumpets. He's been on the game three years, and he's just about as near to making a pull as he ever was."

"Jeff, isn't there danger?" Her voice was very serious.

"Isn't there always danger? No more danger than usual," he said. "They can't touch me. Don't worry! I've covered myself so that they can't see me for overcoats! Once the stuff's printed, they can never put it back on me."

"Once it's printed." She nodded slowly. "Then you *are* the Big Printer, Jeff?"

"Talk about something else," he said.

When Emanuel returned, as he did soon after, Lila met him at the gate and told him of Reeder's visit. To her surprise, he took almost the same view as Jeff had taken.

"He's a fool, but straight—up to five thousand, anyway. No man is straight when you reach his figure."

"But why did he come to Jeff?" she asked.

"Doesn't everybody in the business know that Jeff's the Big Printer? Haven't they been trying to put it on him for years? Of course he came. It was his last, despairing stroke. How's the boy?" he asked.

"He's all right, but a little touchy."

"Of course he's a little touchy," said Emanuel indignantly. "You don't suppose he's going to get better in a day, do you? The club's running again."

"Has it been closed?"

"It hasn't exactly been closed, but it has been unpopular," he said, showing his teeth in that smile of his. "Listen." He caught her arm on the edge of the lawn. "Get your mind off that shooting, will you? I'll fix the man responsible for that."

"Do you know?" she asked.

It was the first time he had ever discussed the matter calmly, for the very mention of the attack upon Jeff had hitherto been sufficient to drive him to an incoherent frenzy.

"Yes, I know," he said gratingly. "It was Peter Kane, but you needn't say anything about that—I'll fix him, I tell you."

"Jeff thinks it was—"

"Never mind what Jeff thinks," he said impatiently. "Do as I tell you."

He sent her into the house to brew him a cup of tea—Emanuel was a great drinker of tea—and in her absence he had something to say to his son.

"Jeff, there's a big call for your stuff," he said. "I've had a letter from Harvey. He says there's another man started in the north of England, and he's turning out pretty good material. But they want yours—they can place half a million on the Continent right away. Jeff, what Harvey says is right. If there's a slackening of supply while you're ill, the busy fellows are going to tumble to you."

"I've thought of that," said Jeffrey. "You can tell anybody who's interested that there'll be a printing next week."

"Are you well enough to go up?" asked his father anxiously.

Jeffrey nodded, and shifted himself more erect, but winced in the process.

"Reeder's been here: did she tell you?"

Emanuel nodded.

"I'm not worried much about Reeder. Down in Dartmoor he's a bogey, but then, they bogey any man they don't know. And they've got all sorts of stories about him. It's very encouraging to get near to the real thing."

They laughed together, and for the rest of the day discussed ways and means.

Jeffrey had said no more than was true when he had told the girl he was well covered. In various parts of the country he had twelve banking accounts, each in a different name, and at one of the safe deposits, an enormous sum in currency, ready for emergency.

"You've got to stop some time, I suppose," said his father, "but it is mighty tempting to carry on with those profits. It's a bigger graft than I ever attempted, Jeff." And his son accepted this respectful tribute with a smirk.

The old man sat, his clasped hands between his knees, staring out over the sea.

"It has got to end some day, and that would be a fine end, but I can't quite see how it could be done."

"What are you talking about?" asked the other curiously.

"I'm thinking about Peter—the respectable Mr. Peter Kane. Not quite so respectable in that girl's eyes as he used to be, but respectable enough to have busies to dinner, and that crook, Johnny Gray—Johnny will marry the girl, Jeff."

Jeffrey Legge winced.

"She can marry the devil so far as I'm concerned," he said.

"But she can't marry without divorcing you. Do you realise that, my son? That's the law. And she can't divorce you without shopping you for bigamy. That's the law too. And the question is, will she delay her action until Johnny's made a bit, or will she start right in? If she gives me just the time I want, Jeff, you'll have your girl and I'll have Peter Kane. She's your wife in the eyes of the law."

There was a significance in his words that made the other man look at him quickly.

"What's the great idea?" he asked.

"Suppose Peter was the Big Printer?" said Emanuel, speaking in a tone that was little above a whisper. "Suppose he was caught with the goods? It could be done. I don't mean by planting the stuff in his house—nobody would accept that; but getting him right on the spot, so that his best friend at Scotland Yard couldn't save him? How's that for an idea?"

"It couldn't be done," said the other immediately.

"Oh, couldn't it?" sneered Emanuel. "You can do any old thing you want, if you make up your mind to do it. Or if you're game to do it."

"That wouldn't get me the girl."

Emanuel turned his head slowly toward his heir.

"If they found the Big Printer, they'll have to find the big printing," he said deliberately. "That means we should all have to skip, and skip lively. We might have a few hours' start, and in these days of aeroplanes, three hours is four hundred miles. Jeff, if we are caught, and they guess I've been in this printing all the time, I shall never see outside again. And you'll go down for life. They can't give you any worse than that—not if you took the girl away with you."

"By force?" asked the other in surprise. The idea had not occurred to him.

The father nodded.

"*If* we have to skip, that's the only thing for you to do, son. It's no offence—remember that. She's your wife." He looked to left and right, to see if there was the faintest shadow of a chance that he would be overheard, and then: "Suppose we ask Peter and his girl *and* Johnny Gray to dinner? A nice little dinner party, eh?"

"Where?" asked the other suspiciously.

"In Room 13," said Emanuel Legge. "In Room 13, Jeff, boy! A nice little dinner. What do you think? And then two whiffs of sleep stuff—"

"You're mad," said the other angrily. "What's the good of talking that way? Do you think he's going to come to dinner and bring his girl? Oh, you're nutty to think it!"

"Trust me," said Emanuel Legge.

CHAPTER 20

Walking down Regent Street one morning, Johnny Gray saw a familiar face—a man standing on the kerb selling penny trinkets The face was oddly familiar, but he had gone on a dozen paces before he could recall where he had seen him before, and turned back The man knew him; at any rate, his uncouth features twisted in a smile

"Good morning, my lord," he said. "What about a toy balloon for the baby?"

"Your name is Fenner, isn't it?" said Johnny with a good-humoured gesture of refusal.

"That's me, Captain. I didn't think you'd recognised me. How's business?"

"Quiet," said Johnny conventionally. "What are you doing?"

The man shrugged his enormous shoulders.

"Selling these, and filling in the time with a little sluicing."

Johnny shook his head reprovingly. "Sluicing" in the argot indicates a curious method of livelihood. In public wash-places, where men strip off their coats to wash their hands for luncheon, there are fine pickings to be had by a man with quick fingers and a knowledge of human nature.

"Did you ever get your towelling[*flogging]?"

"No," said the other contemptuously and with a deep growl. "I knew they couldn't, that's why I coshed the screw. I was too near my time. If I ever see old man Legge, by God I'll—"

Jimmy raised his finger. A policeman was strolling past, and was eyeing the two suspiciously. Apparently, if he regarded Fenner with disfavour, Johnny's respectability redeemed the association.

"Poor old 'flattie'!" said Fenner as the officer passed. "What a life!"

The man looked him up and down amusedly.

"You seem to have struck it, Gray," he said, with no touch of envy. "What's your graft?"

Johnny smiled faintly.

"It is one you'll find difficult to understand, Fenner. I am being honest!"

"That's certainly a new one on me," said the other frankly. "Have you seen old Emanuel?" His voice was now quite calm. "Great fellow, Emanuel! And young Emanuel—Jeffrey—what a lad!"

There was a glint in his eyes as he scrutinised Johnny that told that young man he knew much more of recent happenings than he was prepared to state. And his next words supported that view.

"You keep away from the Legge lot, Captain," he said earnestly. "They are no good to anybody, and least of all to a man who's had an education like yours. I owe Legge one, and I'll get him, but I'm not thinking about that so much as young Jeff. You're the fellow he would go after, because you dress like a swell and you look like a swell—the very man to put 'slush' about without anybody tumbling."

"The Big Printer, eh?" said Johnny, with that quizzical smile of his.

"The Big Printer," repeated the other gravely. "And he *is* a big printer. You hear all sorts of lies down on the moor, but that's true. Jeff's got the biggest graft that's ever been worked in this country. They'll get him sooner or later, because there never was a crook game yet that hadn't got a squeak about it somewhere. And the squeak has started, judging by what I can read in the papers. Who shot him?" he asked bluntly.

Johnny shook his head.

"That is what is known as a mystery," he said, and, seeing the man's eyes keenly searching his face, he laughed aloud. "It wasn't me, Fenner. I'll assure you on that point. And as to me being a friend of Jeff"—he made a wry little face—"that isn't like me either. How are you off for money?"

"Rotten," said the other laconically, and Johnny slipped a couple of Treasury notes on to the tray.

He was turning away when the man called him back.

"Keep out of boob," he said significantly. "And don't think I'm handing round good advice. I'm not thinking of Dartmoor. There are other boobs that are worse—I can tell you that, because I've seen most of them."

He gathered up the money on the tray without so much as a word of thanks, and put it in his waistcoat pocket.

"Keytown Jail is the worst prison in England," he said, not looking at his benefactor but staring straight ahead. "The very worst—don't forget that, Gray. Keytown Prison is the worst boob in England; and if you ever find yourself there, do something to get out. So-long!"

The mentality of the criminal had been a subject for vicarious study during Johnny's stay in Dartmoor, and he mused on the man's words as he continued his walk along Regent Street. Here was a man offering advice which he himself had never taken. The moral detachment of old lags was no new phenomenon to Johnny. He had listened for hours to the wise admonitions and warnings of convicts, who would hardly be free from the fusty cell of the prison before they would be planning new villainies, new qualifications for their return.

He had never heard of Keytown Jail before, but it was not remarkable that Fenner should have some special grudge against a particular jail. The criminal classes have their likes and their dislikes; they loathed Wandsworth and preferred Pentonville, or vice versa, for no especial reason. There were those who swore by Parkhurst; others regarded Dartmoor as home, and bitterly resented any suggestion that they should be transferred to the island prison.

So musing, he bumped into Craig. The collision was not accidental, for Craig had put himself in the way of the abstracted young man.

"What are you planning, Johnny—a jewel robbery, or just ringing the changes on the Derby favourite?"

Johnny chuckled.

"Neither. I was at that moment wondering what there was particularly bad about Keytown Jail. Where is Keytown Jail, by the way?"

"Keytown? I don't remember—oh, yes, I do. Just outside Oxford. Why?"

"Somebody was telling me it was the worst prison in England."

"They are all the worst, Johnny," said Craig. "And if you're thinking out a summer holiday, I can't recommend either. Keytown was pretty bad," he admitted. "It is a little country jail, but it is no longer in the Prison Commissioners' hands. They sold it after the war, when they closed down so many of these little prisons. The policy now is to enlarge the bigger places and cut out these expensive little boobs that cost money to staff. They closed Hereford Jail in the same way, and half a dozen others, I should think. So you needn't bother about Keytown," he smiled bleakly. "One of your criminal acquaintances has been warning you, I guess?"

"You've guessed right," said Johnny, and advanced no information, knowing that, if Craig continued his walk, he would sooner or later see the toy pedlar.

"Mr. Jeffrey Legge is making a good recovery," said the detective, changing the subject; "and there are great rejoicings at Scotland Yard. If there is one man we want to keep alive until he is hanged in a scientific and lawful manner, it is Mr. Jeffrey Legge. I know what you're going to say—we've got nothing on him. That is true. Jeffrey has been too clever for us. He has got his father skinned to death in that respect. He makes no mistakes—a rare quality in a forger; he carries no 'slush,' keeps none in his lodgings. I can tell you that, because we've pulled him in twice on suspicion, and searched him from occiput to *tendo achilles*. Forgive the anatomical terms, but anatomy is my hobby. Hallo!"

He was looking across the street at a figure which was not unfamiliar to Johnny. Mr. Reeder wore a shabby frock-coat and a somewhat untidy silk hat on the back of his head. Beneath his arm he carried a partially furled umbrella. His hands, covered in grey cotton gloves (at a distance Johnny thought they were *suède*) were clasped behind him. His spectacles were, as usual, so far down his nose that they seemed in danger of slipping over.

"Do you know that gentleman?"

"Man named Reeder, isn't it? He's a busy.'"

Craig's lips twitched.

"He's certainly a busy' of sorts," he said dryly, "but not of our sort."

"He is a bank-man, isn't he?" asked Johnny, watching Mr. Reeder's slow and awkward progress.

"He is in the employ of the bank," said the detective, "and he's not such a fool as he looks. I happen to know. He was down seeing young Legge yesterday. I was curious enough to put a man on to trail him. And he knows more about young Legge than I gave him credit for."

When Johnny parted from the detective, Mr. Reeder had passed out of sight. Crossing Piccadilly Circus, however, he saw the elderly man waiting in a bus queue, and interestedly stood and watched him until the bus arrived and Mr. Reeder boarded the machine and disappeared into its interior. As the bus drew away, Johnny raised his eyes to the destination board and saw that it was Victoria.

"I wonder," said Johnny, speaking his thought aloud.

For Victoria is the railway station for Horsham.

CHAPTER 21

Mr Reeder descended from the bus at Victoria Station, bought a third-class return ticket to Horsham, and, going on to the bookstall, purchased a copy of the *Economist* and the *Poultry World*, and, thus fortified for the journey, passed through the barrier, and, finding an empty carriage, ensconced himself in one corner From thence onward, until the train drew into Horsham Station, he was apparently alternately absorbed in the eccentricities of Wyandottes and the fluctuations of the mark

There were many cabs at the station, willing and anxious to convey him to his destination for a trifling sum; but apparently Mr. Reeder was deaf to all the urgent offers which were made to him, for he looked through the taxi-men, or over their heads, as though there were no such things as grimy mechanicians or drivers of emaciated horses; and, using his umbrella as a walking-stick, he set out to walk the distance intervening between the station and Peter Kane's residence.

Peter was in his snuggery, smoking a meditative cigar, when Barney came in with the news.

"There's an old guy wants to see you, Peter. I don't know who he is, but he says his name's Reeder."

Peter's brows met.

"Reeder?" he said sharply. "What sort of man is he?"

"An old fellow," said Barney. "Too shaky for a busy.' He looks as if he's trying to raise subscriptions for the old chapel organ."

It was not an unfair description, as Peter knew.

"Bring him here, Barney, and keep your mouth shut. And bear in mind that this is the busiest busy' you are ever likely to meet."

"A copper?" said Barney incredulously.

Peter nodded.

"Where's Marney?" he asked quickly.

"Up in her boojar," said Barney with relish. "She's writing letters. She wrote one to Johnny. It started 'Dear old boy.'"

"How do you know?" asked Peter sharply.

"Because I read it," said Barney without shame. "I'm a pretty good reader: I can read things upside down, owing to me having been in the printing business when I was a kid."

"Bring in Mr. Reeder," interrupted Peter ominously. "And remember, Barney, that if ever I catch you reading anything of mine upside down, you *will* be upside down! And don't argue."

Barney left the room, uttering a mechanical defiance which such threats invariably provoked.

Mr. Reeder came in, his shabby hat in one hand, his umbrella in the other, and a look of profound unhappiness on his face.

"*Good* morning, Mr. Kane," he said, laying down his impedimenta. "What a beautiful morning it is for a walk! It is a sin and a shame to be indoors on a day like this. Give me a garden, with roses, if I may express a preference, and just a faint whiff of heliotrope…"

"You'd like to see me in the garden, eh?" said Peter. "Perhaps you're wise."

Barney, his inquisitive ears glued to the keyhole, cursed softly.

"I was in a garden yesterday," murmured Mr. Reeder, as they walked across the lawn toward the sunken terraces. "Such a lovely garden! One bed was filled with blue flowers. There is something about a blue flower that brings a lump into my throat. Rhododendrons infuriate me: I have never understood why. There is that about a clump of rhododendrons which rouses all that is evil in my nature. Daffodils, on the other hand, and especially daffodils intermingled with hyacinths, have a most soothing effect upon me. The garden to which I refer had the added attraction of being on the edge of the sea—a veritable Garden of Eden, Mr. Kane, although"—he wagged his head from side to side disparagingly—"there were more snakes than is customary. There was a snake in a chair, and a snake who was posting letters in the village, and another official snake who was hiding behind a clump of bushes and had followed me all the way from London—sent, I think, by that misguided gentleman, Mr. Craig."

"Where were you, Mr. Reeder?"

"At a seaside villa, a beautiful spot. A truly earthly paradise," sighed Mr. Reeder. "The very place an intelligent man would go to if he were convalescent, and the gentleman on the chair was certainly convalescent."

"You saw Jeff Legge, eh? Sit down."

He pointed to the marble bench where Johnny had sat and brooded unhappily on a certain wedding day.

"I think not," said Mr. Reeder, shaking his head as he stared at the marble seat. "I suffer from rheumatism, with occasional twinges of sciatica. I think I would rather walk with you, Mr. Kane." He glanced at the hedge. "I do not like people who listen. Sometimes one listens and hears too much. I heard the other day of a very charming man who happened to be standing behind a bush, and heard the direful character of his son-in-law revealed. It was not good for him to hear so much."

Peter knew that the man was speaking about him, but gave no sign.

"I owe you something, Mr. Reeder, for the splendid way you treated my daughter—"

Mr. Reeder stopped him with a gesture.

"A very charming girl. A very lovely girl," he said with mild enthusiasm. "And so interested in chickens! One so seldom meets with women who take a purely sincere interest in chickens."

They had reached a place where it was impossible they could be overheard. Peter, who realised that the visitor would not have called unless he had something important to say, waited for the next move. Mr. Reeder returned to the subject of eavesdropping.

"My friend—if I may call him my friend—who learnt by accident that his son-in-law was an infernal rascal—if you will excuse that violent expression—might have got himself into serious trouble, very serious trouble." He shook his head solemnly. "For you see," he went on, "my friend—I do hope he will allow me to call him my friend?—has something of a criminal past, and all his success has been achieved by clever strategy. Now, was it clever strategy"—he did not look at Peter, and his faded eyes surveyed the landscape gloomily—"was it clever of my friend to convey to Mr. Emanuel Legge the astounding information that at a certain hour, in a certain room—I think its number was thirteen, but I am not sure—Mr. John Gray was meeting Mr. J.G. Reeder to convey information which would result in Emanuel Legge's son going to prison for a long period of penal servitude? Was it wise to forge the handwriting of one of Emanuel Legge's disreputable associates, and induce the aforesaid Emanuel to mount the fire-escape at the Highlow Club and shoot, as he thought, Mr. John Gray, who wasn't Mr. Gray at all, but his own son? I ask you, was it wise?"

Peter did not answer.

"Was it discreet, when my friend went to the hotel where his daughter was staying, and found her gone, to leave a scribbled note on the floor, which conveyed to Mr. Jeffrey Legge the erroneous information that the young lady was meeting Johnny Gray in Room 13 at nine-thirty? I admit," said Mr. Reeder handsomely, "that by these clever manœuvres, my friend succeeded in getting Jeffrey Legge just where he wanted him at the proper time; for Jeffrey naturally went to the Highlow Club in order to confront and intimidate his wife. You're a man of the world, Mr. Kane, and I am sure you will see how terribly indiscreet my friend was. For Jeffrey might have been killed." He sighed heavily. "His precious life might have been lost; and if the letters were produced at the trial, my friend himself might have been tried for murder."

He dusted the arm of his frock-coat tenderly.

"The event had the elements of tragedy," he said, "and it was only by accident that Jeff's face was turned away from the door; and it was only by accident that Emanuel was not seen going out. And it was only by the sheer-est and cleverest perjury that Johnny Gray was not arrested."

"Johnny was not there," said Peter sharply.

"On the contrary, Johnny was there—please admit that he was there?" pleaded Mr. Reeder. "Otherwise, all my theories are valueless. And a gentle-man in my profession hates to see his theories suffer extinction."

"I'll not admit anything of the sort," said Peter sharply. "Johnny spent that evening with a police officer. It must have been his double."

"His treble perhaps," murmured the other. "Who knows? Humanity re-sembles, to a very great extent, the domestic fowl, *gallus domesticus*. One man resembles another—it is largely a matter of plumage."

He looked up to the sky as though he were seeking inspiration from heaven itself.

"Mr. Jeffrey Legge has not served you very well, Mr. Kane," he said. "In fact, I think he has served you very badly. He is obviously a person without principle or honour, and deserves anything that may come to him."

Peter waited, and suddenly the man brought his eyes to the level of his.

"You must have heard, in the course of your travels, a great deal about Mr. Legge?" he suggested. "Possibly more has come to you since this unfor-tunate—indeed, dastardly—happening, of which I cannot remind you with-out inflicting unnecessary pain. Now, Mr. Kane, don't you think that you would be rendering a service to human society if—"

"If I squeaked," said Peter Kane quietly. "I'll put your mind at rest on that subject immediately. I know nothing of Jeffrey Legge except that he's a blackguard. But if I did, if I had the key to his printing works, if I had evi-dence in my pocket of his guilt—" he paused.

"And if you had all these?" asked Mr. Reeder gently.

"I should not squeak," said Peter with emphasis, "because that is not the way. A squeak is a squeak, whether you do it in cold blood or in the heat of temper."

Again Mr. Reeder sighed heavily, took off his glasses, breathed on them and polished them with gentle vigour, and did not speak until he had replaced them.

"It is all very honourable," he said sadly. "This—er—faith and—er—integrity.... Again the poultry parallel comes to my mind. Certain breeds of chickens hold together and have nothing whatever to do with other breeds, and, though they may quarrel amongst themselves, will fight to the death for one another. Your daughter is well, I trust?"

"She is very well," said Peter emphatically, "surprisingly so. I thought she would have a bad time—here she is." He turned at that moment and waved his hand to the girl, who was coming down the steps of the terrace. "You know Mr. Reeder?" said Peter as the girl came smiling toward the chicken expert with outstretched hand.

"Why, of course I know him," she said warmly. "Almost you have per-suaded me to run a poultry farm!"

"You might do worse," said Mr. Reeder gravely. "There are very few women who take an intelligent interest in such matters. Men are ever so much more interested in chickens."

Peter looked at him sharply. There was something in his tone, a glint of unsuspected humour in his eyes, that lit and died in a second, and Peter Kane was nearer to understanding the man at that moment than he had ever been before.

And here Peter took a bold step.

"Mr. Reeder is a detective," he said, "employed by the banks to try and track down the people who have been putting so many forged notes on the market."

"A detective!"

Her eyes opened wide in surprise, and Mr. Reeder hastened to disclaim the appellation.

"Not a detective. I beg of you not to misunderstand, Miss Kane. I am merely an investigator, an inquiry agent, not a detective. 'Detective' is a term which is wholly repugnant to me. I have never arrested a man in my life, nor have I authority to do so."

"At any rate, you do not look like a detective, Mr. Reeder," smiled the girl.

"I thank you," said Mr. Reeder gratefully. "I should not wish to be mis-taken for a detective. It is a profession which I admire, but do not envy."

He took from his pocket a large note-case and opened it. Inside, fastened by a rubber band in the centre, was a thick wad of bank-notes. Seeing them, Peter's eyebrows rose.

"You're a bold man to carry all that money about with you, Mr. Reeder," he said.

"Not bold," disclaimed the investigator. "I am indeed a very timid man."

He slipped a note from under the elastic band and handed it to his won-dering host. Peter took it.

"A fiver," he said.

Mr. Reeder took another. Peter saw it was a hundred before he held it in his hand.

"Would you cash that for me?"

Peter Kane frowned.

"What do you mean?"

"Would you cash it for me?" asked Mr. Reeder. "Or perhaps you have no change? People do not keep such large sums in their houses."

"I'll change it for you with pleasure," said Peter, and was taking out his own note-case when Mr. Reeder stopped him with a gesture.

"Forged," he said briefly.

Peter looked at the note in his hand.

"Forged? Impossible! That's a good note."

He rustled it scientifically and held it up to the light. The watermark was perfect. The secret marks on the face of the note which he knew very well were there. He moistened the corner of the note with his thumb.

"You needn't trouble," said Reeder. "It answers all the tests."

"Do you mean to tell me this is 'slush'—I mean a forgery?"

The other nodded, and Peter examined the note again with a new interest. He who had seen so much bad money had to admit that it was the most perfect forgery he had ever handled.

"I shouldn't have hesitated to change that for you. Is all the other money the same?"

Again the man nodded.

"But is that really bad money?" asked Marney, taking the note from her father. "How is it made?"

Before the evasive answer came she guessed. In a flash she pieced together the hints, the vague scraps of gossip she had heard about the Big Printer.

"Jeffrey Legge!" she gasped, going white. "Oh!"

"Mr. Jeffrey Legge," nodded Reeder. "Of course we can prove nothing. Now perhaps we can sit down."

It was he who suggested that they should go back to the garden seat. Not until, in his furtive way, he had circumnavigated the clump of bushes that hid the lawn from view did he open his heart.

"I am going to tell you a lot, Mr. Kane," he said, "because I feel you may be able to help me, in spite of your principles. There are two men who could have engraved this note, one man who could manufacture the paper. Anybody could print it—anybody, that is to say, with a knowledge of printing. The two men are Lacey and Burns. They have both been in prison for forgery; they were both released ten years ago, and since then have not been seen. The third man is a paper maker, who was engaged in the bank-note works at Wellington. He went to penal servitude for seven years for stealing bank-note paper. He also has been released a very considerable time, and he also has vanished."

"Lacey and Burns? I have heard of them. What is the other man's name?" asked Peter.

Mr. Reeder told him.

"Jennings? I never heard of him."

"You wouldn't, because he is the most difficult type of criminal to track. In other words, he is not a criminal in the ordinary sense of the word. I am satisfied that he is on the Continent because, to be making paper, it is necessary that one should have the most up-to-date machinery. The printing is done here."

"Where?" asked the girl innocently, and for the first time she saw Mr. Reeder smile.

"I want this man very badly, and it is a matter of interest for you, young lady, because I could get him tomorrow—for bigamy." He saw the girl flush. "Which I shall not do. I want Jeff the Big Printer, not Jeff the bigamist. And oh, I want him badly!"

A sound of loud coughing came from the lawn, and Barney appeared at the head of the steps.

"Anybody want to see Emanuel Legge?"

They looked at one another.

"I don't want to see him," said Mr. Reeder decidedly. He nodded at the girl. "And you don't want to see him. I fear that leaves only you, Mr. Kane."

CHAPTER 22

Peter was as cool as ice when he came into the drawing-room and found Emanuel examining the pictures on the wall with the air of a connoisseur He turned, and beamed a benevolent smile upon the man he hated

"I didn't think you'd come here again, Legge," said Peter with dangerous calm.

"Didn't you, now?" Emanuel seemed surprised. "Well, why not? And me wanting to fix things up, too! I'm surprised at you, Peter."

"You'll put nothing right," said the other. "The sooner you recognise that fact and clear, the better it will be for everybody."

"If I'd known," Emanuel went on, unabashed, "if I'd only dreamt that the young woman Jeffrey had taken up with was your daughter, I would have stopped it at once, Peter. The boy had been brought up straight and never had met you. It is funny the number of straight people that never met Peter Kane. Of course, if he'd been on the crook, he'd have known at once. Do you think my boy would have married the daughter of a man who twisted his father? Is it likely, Peter? However, it's done now, and what's done can't be undone. The girl's fond of him, and he's fond of the girl—"

"When you've finished being comic, you can go," said Peter. "I never laugh before lunch."

"Don't you, Peter? And not after? I've come at a very bad time, it seems to me. Now listen, Peter. Let's talk business."

"I've no business with you." Peter opened the door.

"Haste was always your weakness, Peter," said Emanuel, not budging from where he stood. "Never lose your temper. I lost my temper once and shot a copper, and did fifteen years for it. Fifteen years, whilst you were sitting here in luxury, entertaining the lords and ladies of the neighbourhood, and kidding 'em you were straight. I'm going to ask you a favour, Peter."

"It is granted before you ask," said the other sardonically.

"I'm going to ask you and Johnny boy to come and have a bit of dinner with me and Jeffrey, and let us fix this thing up. You're not going to have this girl brought into the divorce court, are you? And you've got to get divorced, whether he's married or whether he isn't. As a matter of fact, he isn't married at all. I never dreamt you'd be such a mug as to fall for the story that Lila was properly married to Jeff. All these girls tell you the same thing. It's vanity, Peter, a human weakness, if I may so describe it."

"Perhaps it was the vanity of the registrar who signed their marriage certificate, and the vanity of the people who witnessed the marriage," said Peter.
"Your son was married to this girl at the Greenwich Registry Office; I've got
a copy of the certificate—you can see it if you like."

Still the smile on Emanuel's face did not fade.

"Ain't you smart?" he said admiringly. "Ain't you the quickest grafter
that ever grafted? Married or not, Peter, the girl's got to go into the court for
the marriage to be—what do you call it?—annulled, that's the word. And she
can't marry till she does. And they'll never annul the marriage until you get
my boy caught for bigamy, and that you won't do, Peter, because you don't
want to advertise what a damned fool you are. Take my advice, come and talk
it over. Bring Johnny with you—"

"Why should I bring Johnny? I can look after myself."

"Johnny's an interested party," said the other. "He's interested in anything to do with Marney, eh?" He chuckled, and for a second Peter Kane had
all his work to maintain his calm.

"I'm not going to discuss Marney with you. I'll meet you and the Printer,
and I don't suppose Johnny will mind either. Though what you can do that
the law can't do, I don't know."

"I can give you evidence that you can't get any other way," said the
other. "The fact is, Peter, my poor boy has realised he's made a mistake. He
married a girl who was the daughter of a respectable gentleman, and when I
broke it to him, Peter, that he'd married into a crook family, he was upset! He
said I ought to have told him."

"I don't know what funny business you're going to try," said Peter Kane,
"but I'm not going to run away from it. You want me to meet you and your
son—where?"

"What about the old Highlow?" suggested Emanuel. "What about Room
13, where a sad accident nearly occurred?"

"Where you shot your son?" asked Peter coolly, and only for a second
did the man's self-possession leave him. His face turned a dusky red and then
a pale yellow.

"I shot my son there, did I? Peter, you're getting old and dopy! You've
been dreaming again, Peter. Shot my son!"

"I'll come to this fool dinner of yours."

"And Marney?" suggested the other.

"Marney doesn't put her foot inside the doors of the Highlow," said Peter calmly. "You're mad to imagine I would allow that. I can't answer for
Johnny, but I'll be there."

"What about Thursday?" suggested the old man.

"Any day will suit me," said Peter impatiently. "What time do you want
us?"

"Half-past eight. Just a snack and a talk. We may as well have a bit of food to make it cheerful, eh, Peter? Remember that dinner we had a few days before we smashed the Southern Bank? That must be twenty years ago. You split fair on that, didn't you? I'll bet you did—I had the money! No taking a million dollars and calling it a hundred and twenty thousand pounds, eh, Peter?"

This time Peter stood by the door, and the jerk of his head told Emanuel Legge that the moment for persiflage had passed.

"I want to settle this matter." The earnestness of his manner did not deceive Peter. "You see, Peter, I'm getting old, and I want to go abroad and take the boy with me. And I want to give him a chance too—a good-looking lad like that ought to have a chance. For I'll tell you the truth—he's a single man."

Peter smiled.

"You can laugh! He married Lila—you've got a record of that, but have you taken a screw at the divorce list? That takes the grin off your face. They were divorced a year after they were married. Lila got tired of the other man and came back to Jeff. You're a looker-up; go and look up that! Ask old Reeder—"

"Ask him yourself," said Peter. "He's in the garden."

He had no sooner said the words than he regretted them. Emanuel was silent for a while.

"So Reeder's here, in the garden, is he? He's come for a squeak. But you can't, because you've nothing to squeak about. What does he want?"

"Why don't you ask him?"

"That fellow spends his life wandering about other people's gardens," grumbled Emanuel.

A disinterested observer might have imagined that Mr. Reeder's passion for horticulture was the only grievance against him.

"He was round my garden yesterday. I dare say he told you? Came worrying poor Jeff to death. But you always were fond of busies, weren't you, Peter? How's your old friend Craig? I can't stand them myself, but then I am a crook. Thursday will suit you, Peter? That gives you six days."

"Thursday will suit me," said Peter. "I hope it will suit you."

As he came back on to the lawn Reeder and the girl were coming into view up the steps, and without preliminary he told them what had passed.

"I fear," said Mr. Reeder, shaking his head sadly, "that Emanuel is not as truthful a man as he might be. There was no divorce. I was sufficiently interested in the case to look up the divorce court records." He rubbed his chin thoughtfully. "I think your dinner party at the Highlow—is that the name?— will be an interesting one," he said. "Are you sure he did not invite me?" And again Peter saw that glint of humour in his eyes.

CHAPTER 23

Mr. Emanuel Legge had a great deal of business to do in London. The closing of the club had sadly interfered with the amenities of the Highlow, for many of its patrons and members were, not unnaturally, reluctant to be found on premises subject, at any moment, to the visitation of inquisitive police officers. Stevens, the porter, had been reinstated, though his conduct, in Emanuel's opinion, had been open to the gravest suspicion. In other ways he was a reliable man, and one whose services were not lightly to be dispensed with. To his surprise, when he had come to admonish the porter, that individual had taken the wind out of his sails by announcing his intention of retiring unless the staff was changed. And he had his way, the staff in question being the elevator boy Benny.

"Benny squeaked on me," said Stevens briefly, "and I'm not going to have a squeaker round."

"He squeaked to me, my friend," said Emanuel, showing his teeth unpleasantly. "He told me you tried to shield Johnny Gray."

"He's a member, ain't he?" asked the porter truculently. "How do I know what members you want put away, and what members you want hidden? Of course, I helped the Captain—or thought I was trying to help him. That's my job."

There was a great deal of logic in this. Benny, the elevator boy, was replaced.

Stepping out of the lift, Emanuel saw the prints of muddy boots in the hall, and they were wet.

"Who is here?" he asked.

"Nobody in particular."

Legge pointed to the footprints.

"Somebody has been here recently," he said.

"They're mine," said Stevens without hesitation. "I went out to get a cab for Monty Ford."

"Are there any mats?" snapped Emanuel.

Stevens did not answer.

There was a great deal of work for Emanuel to do. For example, there was the matter of a certain house in Berkeley Square to be cleared off. Though he was no longer in active work, he did a lot of crooked financing, and the house had been taken with his money. It was hired furnished for a year, and it was the intention of his associates to run an exclusive gambling club. Unfortunately, the owner, who had a very valuable collection of paintings and old jewellery, discovered the character of the new tenant (a dummy of Legge's) and had promptly cancelled the agreement. Roughly, the venture had cost Emanuel a thousand, and he hated losing good money.

It was late that night when he left the club. He was sleeping in town, intending to travel down to his convalescent son by an early train in the morning. It had been raining heavily, and the street was empty when he went out of the club, pulling the collar of his macintosh about his neck.

He had taken two strides when a man stepped out of the shadow of a doorway and planted himself squarely in his path. Emanuel's hand dropped to his pocket, for he was that rarest variety of criminal, an English gunman.

"Keep your artillery out of action, Legge," said a voice that was strangely familiar.

He peered forward, but in the shadow he could not distinguish the stranger's face.

"Who are you?"

"An old friend of yours," was the reply. "Don't tell me you've forgotten all your pals! Why, you'll be passing a screw in the street one of these days without touching your hat to him."

And then it dawned upon Emanuel.

"Oh… you're Fenner, aren't you?"

"I'm Fenner," admitted the man. "Who else could I be? I've been waiting to see you, Mr. Emanuel Legge. I wondered if you would remember a fellow you sent to the triangle… fifteen lashes I had. You've never had a 'bashing,' have you, Legge? It's not so nice as you'd think. When they'd took me back to my cell and put that big bit of lint on my shoulder, I laid on my face for a week. Naturally, that interfered with my sleeping, though it helped me a whole lot to think. And what I thought was this, Emanuel, that a thousand a stroke wouldn't be too much to ask from the man who got it for me."

Legge's lip twisted in a sneer.

"Oh, it's 'the black' you're after, is it? Fifteen thousand pounds—is that your price?"

"I could do a lot with fifteen thousand, Legge. I can go abroad and have a good time—maybe, take a house in the country."

"What's the matter with Dartmoor?" snarled Emanuel. "You'll get no fifteen thousand from me—not fifteen thousand cents, not fifteen thousand grains of sand. Get out of my way!"

He lurched forward, and the man slipped aside. He had seen what was in the old man's hand.

Legge turned as he passed, facing him and walking sideways, alert to meet any attempt which was launched.

"That's a pretty gun of yours, Legge," drawled the convict. "Maybe I shall meet you one of these days when you won't be in a position to pull it."

A thought struck Emanuel Legge, and he walked slowly back to the man, and his tone was mild, even conciliatory.

"What's the good of making a fuss, Fenner? I didn't give you away. Half a dozen people saw you cosh that screw."

"But half a dozen didn't come forward, did they?" asked Fenner wrathfully. "You were the only prisoner; there was not a screw in sight."

"That's a long time ago," said Emanuel after a pause. "You're not going to make any trouble now, are you? Fifteen thousand pounds is out of the question. It is ridiculous to ask me for that. But if a couple of hundred will do you any good, why, I'll send it to you."

"I'll have it now," said Fenner.

"You won't have it now, because I haven't got it," replied Emanuel. "Tell me where you're to be found, and I'll send a boy along with it in the morning."

Fenner hesitated. He was surprised even to touch for a couple of hundred.

"I'm staying at Rowton House, Wimborne Street, Pimlico."

"In your own name?"

"In the name of Fenner," the other evaded, "and that's good enough for you."

Emanuel memorised the address.

"It will be there at ten o'clock," he said. "You're a mug to quarrel with me. I could put you on to a job where you could have made not fifteen, but twenty thousand."

All the anger had died out of the burglar's tone when he asked:

"Where?"

"There's a house in Berkeley Square," said Emanuel quickly, and gave the number.

It was providential that he had remembered that white elephant of his. And he knew, too, that at that moment the house was empty but for a caretaker.

"Just wait here," he said, and went back into the club and to his little office on the third floor.

Opening a drawer of his desk, he took out a small bunch of keys, the duplicates that had been made during the brief period that the original keys had been in his possession. He found Fenner waiting where he had left him.

"Here are the keys. The house is empty. One of our people borrowed the keys and got cold feet at the last minute. There's about eight thousand pounds' worth of jewellery in a safe—you can't miss it. It is in the principal drawing-room—in show cases—go and take a look at it. And there's plate worth a fortune."

The man jingled the keys in his hand.

"Why haven't you gone after it, Emanuel?"

"Because it's not my graft," said Emanuel. "I'm running straight now. But I want my cut, Fenner. Don't run away with any idea that you're getting this for nothing. You've got a couple of nights to do the job; after that, you haven't the ghost of a chance, because the family will be coming back."

"But why do you give it to me?" asked Fenner, still suspicious.

"Because there's nobody else," was the almost convincing reply. "It may be that the jewellery is not there at all," went on Emanuel frankly. "It may have been taken away. But there is plenty of plate. I wouldn't have given it to you if I'd got the right man—I doubt whether I'm going to get my cut from you."

"You'll get your cut," said the other roughly. "I'm a fool to go after this, knowing what a squeaker you are, but I'll take the risk. If you put a point on me over this, Emanuel, I'll kill you. And I mean it."

"I'm sick of getting news about my murder," said Emanuel calmly. "If you don't want to do it, leave it. I'll send you up a couple of hundred in the morning, and that's all I'll do for you. Give me back those keys."

"I'll think about it," said the man, and turned away without another word.

It was one o'clock, and Emanuel went back to the club, working the automatic lift himself to the second floor.

"Everybody gone, Stevens?" he asked.

The porter stifled a yawn and shook his head.

"There's a lady and a gentleman"—he emphasised the word—"in No. 8. They've been quarrelling since nine o'clock. They ought to be finished by now."

"Put my office through to the exchange," said Emanuel.

Behind the porter's desk was a small switchboard, and he thrust in the two plugs. Presently the disc showed him that Emanuel was through.

Mr. Legge had many friends amongst the minor members of the Criminal Investigation Department. They were not inexpensive acquaintances, but they could on occasion be extremely useful. That night, in some respects, Emanuel's luck was in, when he found Sergeant Shilto in his office. There had been a jewel theft at one of the theatres, which had kept the sergeant busy.

"Is that you, Shilto?" asked Legge in a low voice. "It's Manileg." He gave his telegraphic address, which also served as a *nom de plume* when such delicate negotiations as these were going through.

"Yes, Mr. Manileg?" said the officer, alert, for Emanuel did not call up police head-quarters unless there was something unusual afoot.

"Do you want a cop—a real one?" asked Legge in a voice little above a whisper. "There's a man named Fenner—"

"The old lag?" asked Shilto. "Yes, I saw him today. What's he doing?"

"He's knocking off a little silver, from 973, Berkeley Square. Be at the front door: you'll probably see him go in. You want to be careful, because he's got a gun. If you hurry, you'll get there in front of him. Good night."

He hung up the receiver and smiled. The simplicity of the average criminal always amused Emanuel Legge.

CHAPTER 24

Peter wrote to tell of the invitation which Legge had extended to him Johnny Gray had the letter by the first post He sat in his big arm-chair, his silk dressing-gown wrapped around him, his chin on his fists; and seeing him thus, the discreet Parker did not obtrude upon his thoughts until Johnny, reading the letter again, tore it in pieces and threw it into the wastepaper-basket

He had a whimsical practice of submitting most of his problems, either in parable form or more directly, to his imperturbable manservant.

"Parker, if you were asked to take dinner in a lion's den, what dress would you wear?"

Parker looked down at him thoughtfully, biting his lip.

"It would largely depend, sir, on whether there were ladies to be present," he said. "Under those extraordinary circumstances, one should wear full dress and a white tie."

Johnny groaned.

"There have been such dinners, sir," Parker hastened to assure him in all seriousness. "I recall that, when I was a boy, a visiting menagerie came to our town, and one of the novelties was a dinner which was served in a den of ferocious lions; and I distinctly remember that the lion-tamer wore a white dress bow and a long tail coat. He also wore top boots," he said after a moment's consideration, "which, of course, no gentleman could possibly wear in evening dress. But then, he was an actor."

"But supposing the lion-tamer had a working arrangement with the lions? Wouldn't you suggest a suit of armour?" asked Johnny without smiling.

Parker considered the problem for a moment.

"That would rather turn it into a fancy-dress affair, sir," he said, "where, of course, any costume is permissible. Personally," he added, "I should never dream of dining in a den of lions under any circumstances."

"That's the answer I've been waiting for; it is the most intelligent thing you've said this morning," said Johnny. "Nevertheless, I shall not follow your excellent advice. I will be dining at the Highlow Club on Thursday. Get me the morning newspaper: I haven't seen it."

He turned the pages apathetically, for the events which were at the moment agitating political London meant nothing in his life. On an inner page he found a brief paragraph which, however, did interest him. It was in the latest news column, and related to the arrest of a burglar, who had been caught red-handed breaking into a house in Berkeley Square. The man had given his name as Fenner. Johnny shook his head sadly. He had no doubt as to the identity of the thief, for burglary was Fenner's graft. Since the news had come in the early hours of the morning, there were no details, and he put the paper aside and fell into a train of thought.

Poor Fenner! He must go back to that hell, which was only better than Keytown Jail. He would be spared the ordeal of Keytown, at any rate, if what Craig had said was true. Glancing at the clock, he saw that it was nearly eleven and jumped up. He was taking Marney to lunch and a *matinée* that day. Peter was bringing her up, and he was to meet them at Victoria.

Since his release from Dartmoor, Johnny had had no opportunity of a quiet talk with the girl, and this promised to be a red-letter day in his life. He had to wait some time, for the train was late; and as he stood in the broad hall, watching with abstracted interest the never-ceasing rush and movement and life about him, he observed, out of the corner of his eye, a man sidling toward him.

Johnny had that sixth sense which is alike the property of the scientist, the detective and the thief. He was immediately sensitive to what he called the approaching spirit, and long before the shabby stranger had spoken to him, he knew that he was the objective. Nearer at hand, he recognised the stranger as a man he had seen in Dartmoor, and remembered that he had come to prison at the same time as Fenner and for the same offence, though he had been released soon after Johnny had passed through that grim gateway.

"I followed you down here, Mr. Gray, but I didn't like to talk to you in the street," said the stranger, apparently immersed in an evening newspaper, and talking, as such men talk, without moving his lips.

Johnny waited, wondering what was the communication, and not doubting that it had to do with Fenner.

"Old Fenner's been 'shopped' by Legge," said the man. "He went to 'knock off' some silver from a house in Berkeley Square, and Shilto was waiting in the hall for him."

"How do you know Legge 'shopped' him?" asked Johnny, interested.

"It was a 'shop' all right," said the other without troubling to explain. "If you can put in a good word for Fenner, he'd be much obliged."

"But, my dear fellow," said John with a little smile, "to whom can I put in a good word? In the present circumstances I couldn't put a word in for my own maiden aunt. I'll see what I can do."

There was no need to tell the furtive man to go. With all a thief's keen perceptions he had seen the eyes of Johnny Gray light up, and with a sidelong glance assured himself as to the cause. Johnny went toward the girl with long strides, and, oblivious to curious spectators and Peter Kane alike, took both her hands in his. Her loveliness always came to him in the nature of a glorious surprise. The grace and poise of her were indefinite quantities that he could not keep exactly in his mind, and inevitably she surpassed his impressions of her.

After he had handed the girl into a taxi, the older man beckoned him aside.

"I'm not any too sure about this Highlow dinner," he said. "Love feasts are not Emanuel's specialities, and there's a kick coming somewhere, Johnny. I hope you're prepared for it?"

Johnny nodded.

"Emanuel isn't usually so obvious," he said. "In fact, the whole thing is so patent and so crude that I can't suspect anything more than an attempt to straighten matters as far as Marney is concerned."

Peter's face clouded.

"There will be no straightening there," he said shortly. "If he has committed bigamy, he goes down for it. Understand that, Johnny. It will be very unpleasant because of Marney's name being dragged into the light, but I'm going through with it."

He turned away with a wave of his hand, and Johnny returned to the girl.

"What is the matter with father?" she asked as the taxi drew out of the station. "He is so quiet and thoughtful these days. I suppose the poor dear's worrying about me, though he needn't, for I never felt happier."

"Why?" asked Johnny, indiscreetly.

"Because—oh, well, because," she said, her face flushing the faintest shade of pink. "Because I'm unmarried, for one thing. I hated the idea, Johnny. You don't know how I hated it. I understand now poor daddy's anxiety to get me married into respectable society." Her sense of humour, always irrepressible, overcame her anxiety. "I wonder if you understand my immoral sense of importance at the discovery that poor father has done so many illegal things! I suppose it is the kink that he has transmitted to me."

"Was it a great shock to you, Marney?" interrupted the young man quietly.

She nodded.

"Yes, but shocks are like blows—they hurt and they fade. It isn't pleasant to be twisted violently to another angle of view. It pains horribly, Johnny. But I think when I found—" She hesitated.

"When you found that I was a thief."

"When I found that you were—oh, Johnny, why did you? You had so many advantages; you were a University man, a gentleman—Johnny, it wasn't big of you. There's an excuse for daddy; he told me about his youth and his struggles and the fearful hardness of living. But you had opportunities that he never had. Easy money isn't good money, is it, Johnny?"

He was silent, and then, with a quick, breath-catching sigh, she smiled again.

"I haven't come out to lecture you, and I shall not even ask you if, for my sake, you will go straight in the future. Because, Johnny"—she dropped a cool palm on the back of his hand—"I'm not going to do anything like the good fairy in the storybooks and try to save you from yourself."

"I'm saved," said Johnny with a quizzical smile. "You're perfectly right: there was no reason why I should be a thief. I was the victim of circumstances. It was possibly the fascination of the game—no, no, it wasn't that. One of these days I will tell you why I left the straight path of virtue. It is a long and curious story."

She made no further reference to his fall, and throughout the lunch was her own gay self. Looking down at her hand, Johnny saw, with satisfaction, that the platinum wedding-ring she had worn had been replaced by a small, plain gold ring, ornamented with a single turquoise, and his breath came faster. He had first met her at a gymkhana, a country fair which had been organised for charity, and the ring had been the prize he had won at a shooting match, one of the gymkhana features—though it was stretching terminology to absurd lengths so to describe the hotch-potch of contests which went to the making of the programme—and had offered it to her as whimsically as it had been accepted. Its value was something under a pound; to Johnny, all the millions in the world would not have given him the joy that its appearance upon her finger gave him now.

After luncheon she returned to the unpleasant side of things.

"Johnny, you're going to be very careful, aren't you? Daddy says that Jeff Legge hates you, and he is quite serious about it. He says that there are no lengths to which Jeffrey and his father will not go to hurt you—and me," she added.

Johnny bent over the table, lowering his voice.

"Marney, when this matter is settled—I mean, the release from your marriage—will you take me—whatever I am?"

She met his eyes steadily and nodded. It was the strangest of all proposals, and Jeffrey Legge, who had watched the meeting at the station, had followed her, and now was overlooking them from one of the balconies of the restaurant, flushed a deeper red, guessing all that that scene meant.

CHAPTER 25

On Thursday afternoon, Emanuel Legge came out of the elevator at the Highlow Club, and, with a curt nod to Stevens, walked up the heavily carpeted corridor, unlocked the door of his tiny office and went in For half an hour he sat before his desk, his hands clasped on the blotting-pad before him, motionless, his mind completely occupied by his thoughts At last he opened his desk, pressed a bell by his side, and he had hardly taken his fingers from the push when the head waiter of the establishment, a tall, unpleasant-looking Italian, came in

"Fernando, you have made all the arrangements about the dinner tonight?"

"Yes," said the man.

"All the finest wines, eh? The best in the house?"

He peered at the waiter, his teeth showing in a smile.

"The very best," said Fernando briskly.

"There will be four: myself and Major Floyd, Mr. Johnny Gray and Peter Kane."

"The lady is not coming?" asked Fernando.

"No, I don't think she'll be dining with us tonight," said Emanuel carefully.

When the waiter had gone, he rose and bolted the door and returned to an idle examination of the desk. He found extraordinary pleasure in opening the drawers and looking through the little works of reference which filled a niche beneath the pigeon-holes. This was Jeffrey's desk, and Jeff was the apple of his eye.

Presently he rose and walked to a nest of pigeon-holes which stood against the wall, and, putting his hand into one, he turned a knob and pulled. The nest opened like a door, exposing a narrow, spiral staircase which led upward and downward. He left the secret door open and pulled down a switch, which gave him light above and below. For a second he hesitated whether he should go up or down, and decided upon the latter course.

At the foot of the stairs was another door, which he opened, passing into the cellar basement of the house. As the door moved, there came to him a wave of air so super-heated that for a moment he found difficulty in breathing. The cellar in which he found himself was innocent of furnishing, except for a table placed under a strong light, and a great, enclosed furnace which was responsible for the atmosphere of the room. It was like a Turkish bath, and he had not gone two or three paces before the perspiration was rolling down his cheeks.

A broad-shouldered, undersized man was sitting at the table, a big book open before him. He had turned at the sound of the key in the door, and now he came toward the intruder. He was a half-caste, and, beyond the pair of blue dungaree trousers, he wore no clothing. His yellow skin and his curiously animal face gave him a particularly repulsive appearance.

"Got the furnace going, eh, Pietro?" said Emanuel mildly, taking off his spectacles to wipe the moisture which had condensed upon the lenses.

Pietro grunted something and, picking up an iron bar, lifted open the big door of the furnace. Emanuel put up his hands to guard his face from the blast of heat that came forth.

"Shut it, shut it!" he said testily, and when this was done, he went nearer to the furnace.

Two feet away there ran a box-like projection, extending from two feet above the floor to the ceiling. A stranger might have imagined that this was an air shaft, introduced to regulate the ventilation. Emanuel was not a stranger. He knew that the shaft ran to the roof, and that it had a very simple explanation.

"That's a good fire you've got, eh, Pietro? You could burn up a man there?"

"Burn anything," growled the other, "but not man."

Emanuel chuckled.

"Scared I'm going to put a murder point on you, are you? Well, you needn't be," he said. "But it's hot enough to melt copper, eh, Pietro?"

"Melt it down to nothing."

"Burnt any lately?"

The man nodded, rubbing his enormous arms caressingly.

"They came last Monday week, after the boss had been shot," said the other. He had a curious impediment in his speech which made his tone harsh and guttural. "The fellows upstairs knew they were coming, so there was nothing to see. The furnace was nearly out."

Emanuel nodded.

"The boss said the furnace was to be kept going for a week," said Pietro complainingly. "That's pretty tough on me, Mr. Legge. I feel sometimes I'd nearly die, the heat's so terrible."

"You get the nights off," said Emanuel, "and there are weeks when you do no work. Tonight I shall want you.... Mr. Jeff has told you?"

The dwarf nodded. Emanuel passed through the door, closing it behind him; and, contrasted with the heat of the room, it seemed that he had walked into an ice wall. His collar was limp, his clothes were sticking to him, as he made his way up the stairs, and, passing the open door of his office, continued until he reached the tiny landing which scarcely gave him foothold. He knocked twice on the door, for of this he had no key. After a pause came an answering knock, a small spy-hole opened and an inquiring and suspicious eye examined him.

When at last the door was opened, he found he was in a small room with a large skylight, heavily barred. At one end of the skylight was a rolled blind, which could be drawn across at night and effectively veil the glare of light which on occasions rose from this room.

The man who grinned a welcome was little and bald. His age was in the region of sixty, and the grotesqueness of his appearance was due less to his shabby attire and diminutive stature than to the gold-rimmed monocle fixed in his right eye.

In the centre of the room was a big table, littered with paraphernalia, ranging from a small microscope to a case filled with little black bottles. Under the brilliant overhead light which hung above the table, and clamped to the wood by glass-headed pins, was an oblong copper plate, on which the engraver had been working—the engraving tool was in his hand as he opened the door.

"Good morning, Lacey. What are you working at now?" asked Emanuel with a benevolent air of patronage appropriate to the proprietor in addressing a favourite workman.

"The new fives," said the other. "Jeff wants a big printing. Jeff's got brains. Anybody else would have said, 'Work from a photographic plate'— you know what that means. After a run of a hundred, the impression goes wrong, and before you know where you are, there's a squeak. But engraving is engraving," he said with pride. "You can get all the new changes without photography. I never did hold with this new method—'boobs' are full of fellows who think they can make slush with a camera and a zinc plate!"

It was good to hear praise of Jeffrey, and Emanuel Legge purred. He examined the half-finished plate through his powerful glasses, and though the art of the engraver was one with which he was not well acquainted, he could admire the fine work which this expert forger was doing.

To the left of the table was an aperture like the opening of a service lift. It was a continuation of the shaft which led from the basement, and it had this value, that, however clever the police might be, long before they could break into the engraver's room all evidence of his guilt would have been flung into the opening and consumed in the furnace fire.

"Jeffrey's idea. What a mind!" said the admiring Lacey. "It reduces risk to what I might term a minimum. It is a pleasure working for Jeff, Mr. Legge. He takes no chances."

"I suppose Pietro is always on the spot?"

Mr. Lacey smiled. He took up a plate from the table and examined it back and front.

"That is one I spoilt this morning," he said. "Spilt some acid on it. Look!"

He went to the opening, put in his hand, and evidently pressed a bell, for a faint tinkle came from the mouth of the shaft. When he withdrew his hand, the plate that it held had disappeared. There came the buzz of a bell from beneath the table.

"That plate's running like water by now," he said. "There's no chance of a squeak if Pietro's all right. Wide! That's Jeffrey! As wide as Broad Street! Why, Mr. Legge, would you believe that I don't know to this day where the stuff's printed? And I'll bet the printer hasn't got the slightest idea where the plates are made. There isn't a man in this building who has got so much as a smell of it."

Emanuel passed down to his own office, a gratified father, and, securely closing the pigeon-hole door, he went out into the club premises to look at Room 13. The table was already laid; a big rose-bowl, overflowing with the choicest blooms, filled the centre; an array of rare glass, the like of which the habitués of the club had never seen on their tables, stood before each plate.

His brief inspection of the room satisfied him, and he returned, not to his office but to Stevens, the porter.

"What's the idea of telling the members that all the rooms are engaged tonight?" asked Stevens. "I've had to put off Lew Brady, and he pays."

"We're having a party, Stevens," said Emanuel, "and we don't want any interruption. Johnny Gray is coming. And you can take that look off your face; if I thought he was a pal of yours, you wouldn't be in this club two minutes. Peter Kane's coming too."

"Looks to me like a rough house," said Stevens. "What am I to do?" he asked sarcastically. "Bring in the police at the first squeal?"

"Bring in your friend from Toronto," snapped Emanuel, and went home to change.

CHAPTER 26

Johnny was the first of the guests to arrive, and Stevens helped him to take off his raincoat As he did so, he asked in a low voice:

"Got a gun, Captain?"

"Never carry one, Stevens. It is a bad habit to get into."

"I never thought you were a mug," said Stevens in the same voice.

"Any man who has been in prison is, *ex officio*, one of the Ancient Order of Muggery," said Johnny, adjusting his bow in the mirror by the porter's desk. "What's going?"

"I don't know," said the other, bending down to wipe the mud from Johnny's boots. "But curious things have happened in No. 13; and don't sit with your back to the buffet. Do you get that?"

Johnny nodded.

He had reached the end of the corridor when he heard the whine of the ascending lift, and stopped. It was Peter Kane, and to him, in a low voice, Johnny passed on the porter's advice.

"I don't think they'll start anything," said Peter under his breath. "But if they do, there's a nurse at Charing Cross Hospital who's going to say: 'What, you here again!'"

As Johnny had expected, his two hosts were waiting in Room 13. The silence which followed their arrival was, for one member of the party, an awkward one.

"Glad to see you, Peter," said Emanuel at last, though he made no pretence of shaking hands. "Old friends ought to keep up acquaintances. There's my boy, Jeffrey. I think you've met him," he said with a grin.

"I've met him," said Peter, his face a mask.

Jeffrey Legge had apparently recovered fully from his unpleasant experience.

"Now sit down, everybody," said Emanuel, bustling around, pulling out the chairs. "You sit here, Johnny."

"I'd rather face the buffet; I like to see myself eat," said Johnny, and, without invitation, sat down in the position he had selected.

Not waiting, Peter seated himself on Johnny's left, and it was Emanuel himself, a little ruffled by this preliminary upset to his plans, who sat with his back to the buffet. Johnny noticed the quick exchange of glances between father and son; he noticed, too, that the buffet carried none of the side dishes for which it was designed, and wondered what particular danger threatened from that end of the room.

By the side of the sideboard, in one corner, hung a long, blue curtain, which, he guessed, hid a door leading to No. 12. Peter, who was better acquainted with the club, knew that No. 12 was the sitting-room, and that the two made one of those suites which were very much in request when a lamb was brought to the killing.

"Now, boys," said Emanuel with spurious joviality, "there is to be no bickering and quarrelling. We're all met round the festive board, and we've nothing to do but find a way out that leaves my boy's good name unsullied, if I may use that word."

"You can use any word you like," said Peter. "It'll take more than a dinner party to restore his tarnished reputation."

"What long words you use, Peter!" said Emanuel admiringly. "It's my own fault that I don't know them, because I had plenty of time to study when I was away 'over the Alps.' Never been over the Alps, have you, Peter? Well, when they call it 'tis?me,' they use the right word. The one thing you've got there is time!"

Peter did not answer, and it was Jeffrey who took up the conversation.

"See here, Peter," he said, "I'm not going to make a song about this business of mine. I'm going to put all my cards on the table. I want my wife."

"You know where Lila is better than I," said Peter. "She's not in my employment now."

"Lila nothing!" retorted Jeffrey. "If you fall for that stuff, you're getting soft. I certainly married Lila, but she was married already, and I can give you proof of it."

The conversation flagged here, for the waiter came in to serve the soup.

"What wine will you have, sir?"

"The same as Mr. Emanuel," said Peter.

Emanuel Legge chuckled softly.

"Think I'm going to 'knock you out,' eh, Peter? What a suspicious old man you are!"

"Water," said Johnny softly when the waiter came to him.

"On the water-wagon, Johnny? That's good. A young man in your business has got to keep his wits about him. I'll have champagne, Fernando, and so will Major Floyd. Nothing like champagne to keep your heart up," he said.

Peter watched, all his senses alert, as the wine came, bubbling and frothing, into the long glasses.

"That will do, Fernando," said Emanuel, watching the proceedings closely.

As the door closed, Johnny could have sworn he heard an extra click.

"Locking us in?" he asked pleasantly, and Emanuel's eyebrows rose.

"Locking you in, Johnny? Why, do you think I'm afraid of losing you, like you're afraid of losing Marney?"

Johnny sipped the glass of water, his eyes fixed on the old man's face. What was behind that buffet? That was the thought which puzzled him. It was a very ordinary piece of furniture, of heavy mahogany, a little shallow, but this was accounted for by the fact that the room was not large, and, in furnishing, the proprietors of the club had of necessity to economise space.

There were two cupboard doors beneath the ledge on which the side dishes should have been standing. Was it his imagination that he thought he saw one move the fraction of an inch?

"Ever been in 'bird' before, Johnny?"

It was Emanuel who did most of the talking.

"I know they gave you three years, but was that your first conviction?"

"That was my first conviction," said Johnny.

The old man looked up at the ceiling, pulling at his chin.

"Ever been in Keytown?" he demanded. "No good asking you, Peter, I know. You've never been in Keytown or any bad boob, have you? Clever old Peter!"

"Let us talk about something else," said Peter. "I don't believe for one moment the story you told me about Lila having been married before. You've told me a fresh lie every time the matter has been discussed. I'm going to give you a show, Emanuel, for old times' sake. You've been a swine, and you've been nearer to death than you know, for, if your plan had come off as you expected it would, I'd have killed you."

Emanuel chuckled derisively.

"Old Peter's going to be a gunman," he said. "And after all the lectures you've given me! I'm surprised at you, Peter. Now I'll tell you what I'm going to do." He rested his elbows on the table and cupped his chin in his hands, his keen eyes, all the keener for the magnification of his spectacles, fixed hardly upon his sometime friend. "By my reckoning, you owe me forty thousand pounds, and I know I'm not going to get it without a struggle. Weigh in with that money, and I'll make things easy for my son's wife." He emphasised the last word.

"You can cut that out!"

It was Jeffrey whose rough interruption checked his father's words.

"There's no money in the world that's going to get Marney from me. Understand that." He brought his hand down with a crash upon the table. "She belongs to me, and I want her, Peter. Do you get it? And what is more, I'm going to take her."

Johnny edged a little farther from the table, and folding his arms across his chest, his lips parted in a smile. His right hand reached for the gun that he carried under his armpit: a little Browning, but a favourite one of Johnny's in such crises as these. For the cupboard door had moved again, and the door of the room was locked: of that he was certain. All this talk of Marney was sheer blind to keep them occupied.

It had long passed the time when the plates should have been cleared and the second course make its appearance. But there was to be no second course at that dinner. Emanuel was speaking chidingly, reproachfully.

"Jeffrey, my boy, you mustn't spoil a good deal," he said. "The truth is—"

And then all the lights of the room went out. Instantly Johnny was on his feet, his back to the wall, his gun fanning the dark.

"What's the game?" asked Peter's voice sharply. "There'll be a real dead man here if you start fooling."

"I don't know," said Emanuel, speaking from the place where he had been. "Ring the bell, Jeff. I expect the switch has gone."

There was somebody else in the room: Johnny felt the presence instinctively—a stealthy somebody who was moving toward him. Holding out one hand, ready to pounce the moment it touched, he waited. A second passed— five seconds—ten seconds—and then the lights went on again.

Peter was also standing with his back to the wall, and in his hand a murderous looking Webley. Jeffrey and his father were side by side in the places they had been when the lights went out. There was no fifth man in the room.

"What's the game?" asked Peter suspiciously.

"The game, my dear Peter? What a question to ask! You don't make me responsible for the fuses, do you? I'm not an electrician. I'm a poor old crook who has done time that other people should have done—that's all," said Emanuel pleasantly. "And look at the hardware! Bad idea, carrying guns. Let an old crook give you a word of advice, Peter," he bantered. "I'm not surprised at Johnny, because he might be anything. Sit down, you damned fools," he said jocularly. "Let's talk."

"I'll talk when you open that door," said Johnny quietly. "And I'll put away my gun on the same condition."

In three strides, Emanuel was at the door. There was a jerk of his wrist, and it flew open.

"Have the door open if you're frightened," he said contemptuously. "I guess it's being in boob that makes you scared of the dark. I got that way myself."

As he had turned the handle, Johnny had heard a second click. He was confident that somebody stood outside the door, and that the words Legge had uttered were intended for the unknown sentry. What was the idea?

Peter Kane was sipping his champagne with an eye on his host. Had he heard the noise, too? Johnny judged that he had. The extinguishing of the lights had not been an accident. Some secret signal had been given, and the lights cut off from the controlling switchboard. The doors of the buffet cupboard were still. Turning his head, Johnny saw that Jeffrey's eyes were fixed on his with a hard concentration which was significant. What was he expecting?

The climax, whatever it might be, was at hand.

"It's a wonder to me, Gray, that you've never gone in for slush." Jeffrey was speaking slowly and deliberately. "It's a good profession, and you can make money that you couldn't dream of getting by faking racehorses."

"Perhaps you will tell me how to start in that interesting profession," said Johnny coolly.

"I'll put it on paper for you, if you like. It'll be easier to make a squeak about. Or, better still, I'll show you how it's done. You'd like that?"

"I don't know that I'm particularly interested, but I'm sure my friend Mr. Reeder—"

"Your friend Mr. Reeder!" sneered the other. "He's a pal of yours too, is he?"

"All law-abiding citizens are pals of mine," said Johnny gravely.

He had put his pistol back in his jacket pocket, and his hand was on it.

"Well, how's this for a start?"

Jeffrey rose from the table and went to the buffet. He bent down and must have touched some piece of mechanism; for, without any visible assistance, the lid of the buffet turned over on some invisible axis, revealing a small but highly complicated piece of machinery, which Johnny recognised instantly as one of those little presses employed by banknote printers when a limited series of notes, generally of a high denomination, were being made.

The audacity of this revelation momentarily took his breath away.

"You could pull that buffet to pieces," continued Jeffrey, "and then not find it."

He pressed a switch, and the largest of the wheels began to spin, and with it a dozen tiny platens and cylinders. Only for a few minutes, and then he cut off the current, pressed the hidden mechanism again, and the machine turned over out of sight, and the two astonished men stared at the very ordinary looking surface of a very ordinary buffet.

"Easy money, eh, Gray?" said Emanuel, with an admiring smirk at his son. "Now listen, boys." His tone grew suddenly practical and businesslike as he came back to his chair. "I want to tell you something that's going to be a lot of good to both of you, and we'll leave Marney out of it for the time being."

Johnny raised his glass of water, still watchful and suspicious.

"The point is—" said Emanuel, and at that moment Johnny took a long sip from the glass.

The liquid had hardly reached his throat when he strove vainly to reject it. The harsh tang of it he recognised, and, flinging the glass to the floor, jerked out his gun.

And then some tremendous force within him jerked at his brain, and the pistol dropped from his paralysed hand.

Peter was on his feet, staring from one to the other.

"What have you done?"

He leapt forward, but before he could make a move, Emanuel sprang at him like a cat. He tried to fight clear, but he was curiously lethargic and weak. A vicious fist struck him on the jaw, and he went down like a log.

"Got you!" hissed Emanuel, glaring down at his enemy. "Got you, Peter, my boy! Never been in boob, have you? I'll give you a taste of it!"

Jeffrey Legge stooped and jerked open the door of the cupboard, and a man came stooping into the light. It was a catlike Pietro, grinning from ear to ear in sheer enjoyment of the part he had played. Emanuel dropped his hand on his shoulder.

"Good boy," he said. "The right stuff for the right man, eh? To every man his dope, Jeff. I knew that this Johnny Gray was going to be the hardest, and if I'd taken your advice and given them both a knock-out, we'd have only knocked out one. Now they know why the lights went out. Pick 'em up."

The little half-caste must have been enormously strong, for he lifted Peter without an effort and propped him into an arm-chair. This done, he picked up the younger man and laid him on the sofa, took a little tin box from his pocket, and, filling a hypodermic syringe from a tiny phial, looked round for instructions.

Jeffrey nodded, and the needle was driven into the unfeeling flesh. This done, he lifted the eyelid of the drugged man and grinned again.

"He'll be ready to move in half an hour," he said. "My knock-out doesn't last longer."

"Could you get him down the fire-escape into the yard?" asked Emanuel anxiously. "He's a pretty heavy fellow, that Peter. You'll have to help him, Jeff boy. The car's in the yard. And, Jeff, don't forget you've an engagement at two o'clock."

His son nodded.

Again the half-caste swung up Peter Kane, and Jeffrey, holding the door wide, helped him to carry the unconscious man through the open window and down the steel stairway, though he needed very little help, for the strength of the man was enormous.

He came back, apparently unmoved by his effort, and hoisted Johnny on to his back. Again unassisted, he carried the young man to the waiting car below, and flung him into the car.

He was followed this time by Jeffrey, wrapped from head to foot in a long waterproof, a chauffeur's cap pulled down over his eyes. They locked both doors of the machine, and Pietro opened the gate and glanced out. There were few people about, and the car swung out and sped at full speed toward Oxford Street.

Closing and locking the gate, the half-caste went up the stairs of the fire-escape two at a time and reported to his gratified master.

Emanuel was gathering the coats and hats of his two guests into a bundle. This done, he opened a cupboard and flung them in, and they immediately disappeared.

"Go down and burn them," he said laconically. "You've done well, Pietro. There's fifty for you tonight."

"Good?" asked the other laconically.

Emanuel favoured him with his benevolent smile. He took the two glasses from which the men had drunk, and these followed the clothes. A careful search of the room brought to light no further evidence of their presence. Satisfied, Emanuel sat down and lit a long, thin cigar. His night's work was not finished. Jeff had left to him what might prove the hardest of all the tasks.

From a small cupboard he took a telephone, and pushed in the plug at the end of a long flex. He had some time to wait for the number, but presently he heard a voice which he knew was Marney's.

"Is that you, Marney?" he asked softly, disguising his voice so cleverly that the girl was deceived.

"Yes, daddy. Are you all right? I've been so worried about you."

"Quite all right, darling. Johnny and I have made a very interesting discovery. Will you tell Barney to go to bed, and will you wait up for me—open the door yourself?"

"Is Johnny coming back with you?"

"No, no, darling; I'm coming alone."

"Are you sure everything is all right?" asked the anxious voice.

"Now, don't worry, my pet. I shall be with you at two o'clock. When you hear the car stop at the gate, come out. I don't want to come into the house. I'll explain everything to you."

"But—"

"Do as I ask you, darling," he said, and before she could reply had rung off.

But could Jeff make it? He would like to go himself, but that would mean the employment of a chauffeur, and he did not know one he could trust. He himself was not strong enough to deal with the girl, and, crowning impossibility, motorcar driving was a mystery—that was one of the accomplishments which a long stay in Dartmoor had denied to him.

But could Jeff make it? He took a pencil from his pocket and worked out the times on the white tablecloth. Satisfied, he put away his pencil, and was pouring out a glass of champagne when there was a gentle tap-tap-tap at the door. He looked up in surprise. The man had orders not under any circumstances to come near Room 13, and it was his duty to keep the whole passage clear until he received orders to the contrary.

Tap-tap-tap.

"Come in," he said.

The door opened. A man stood in the doorway. He was dressed in shabby evening clothes; his bow was clumsily tied; one stud was missing from his white shirt-front.

"Am I intruding upon your little party?" he asked timidly.

Emanuel said nothing. For a long time he sat staring at this strange apparition. As if unconscious of the amazement and terror he had caused, the visitor sought to readjust his frayed shirt-cuffs, which hung almost to the knuckles of his hands. And then:

"Come in, Mr. Reeder," said Emanuel Legge a little breathlessly.

CHAPTER 27

Mr. Reeder sidled into the room apologetically, closing the door behind him.

"All alone, Mr. Legge?" he asked. "I thought you had company?"

"I had some friends, but they've gone."

"Your son gone, too?" Reeder stared helplessly from one corner of the room to the other. "Dear me, this is a disappointment, a great disappointment."

Emanuel was thinking quickly. In all probability the shabby detective had been watching the front of the house, and would know that they had not left that way. He took a bold step.

"They left a quarter of an hour ago. Peter and Johnny went down the fire-escape—my boy's car was in the yard. We never like to have a car in front of the club premises; people talk so much. And after the publicity we've had—"

Mr. Reeder checked him with a mild murmur of agreement.

"That was the car, was it? I saw it go and wondered what it was all about—Number XC. 9712, blue painted limousine—Daimler—I may be wrong, but it seemed like a Daimler to me; I know so little about motorcars that I could be very easily mistaken, and my eyesight is not as good as it used to be."

Emanuel cursed him under his breath.

"Yes, it was a Daimler," he said, "one we bought cheap at the sales."

The absent-minded visitor's eyes were fixed on the table.

"Took their wine-glasses with them?" he asked gently. "I think it is a pretty custom, taking souvenirs of a great occasion. I'm sure they were very happy."

How had he got in, wondered Emanuel? Stevens had strict orders to stop him, and Fernando was at the end of the L-shaped passage. As if he divined the thought that was passing through Legge's mind, Mr. Reeder answered the unspoken question.

"I took the liberty of coming up the fire-escape, too," he said. "It was an interesting experience. One is a little old to begin experiments, and I am not the sort of man that cares very much for climbing, particularly at night."

Following the direction of his eyes, Emanuel saw that a small square of the rusty trousers had been worn, and through the opening a bony white knee.

"Yes, I came up the fire-escape, and fortunately the window was open. I thought I would give you a pleasant surprise. By the way, the escape doesn't go any higher than this floor? That is curious, because, you know, my dear Mr. Legge, it might well happen, in the event of fire, that people would be driven to the roof. If I remember rightly, there is nothing on the roof but a square superstructure—store-room, isn't it? Let me think. Yes, it's a store-room, I'm sure."

"The truth is," interrupted Emanuel, "I had two old acquaintances here, Johnny Gray and Peter Kane. I think you know Peter?"

The other inclined his head gently.

"And they got just a little too merry. I suppose Johnny's not used to wine, and Peter's been a teetotaller for years." He paused. "In fact, they were rather the worse for drink."

"That's very sad." Mr. Reeder shook his head. "Personally, I am a great believer in prohibition. I would prohibit wine and beer, and crooks and forgers, tale-tellers, poisoners"—he paused at the word—"druggers would be a better word," he said. "They took their glasses with them, did they? I hope they will return them. I should not like to think that people I—er—like would be guilty of so despicable a practice as—er—the petty theft of—er—wine-glasses."

Again his melancholy eyes fell on the table.

"And they only had soup! It is very unusual to get bottled before you've finished the soup, isn't it? I mean, in respectable circles," he added apologetically.

He looked back at the open door over his spectacles.

"I wonder," he mused, "how they got down that fire-escape in the dark in such a sad condition?"

Again his expressionless eyes returned to Emanuel.

"If you see them again, will you tell them that I expect both Mr. Kane and Mr. Johnny—what is his name?—Gray, that is it! to keep an appointment they made with me for tomorrow morning? And that if they do not turn up at my house at ten o'clock…"

He stopped, pursing up his lips as though he were going to whistle. Emanuel wondered what was coming next, and was not left long in doubt.

"Did you feel the cold very much in Dartmoor? They tell me that the winters are very trying, particularly for people of an advanced age. Of course," Mr. Reeder went on, "one can have friends there; one can even have relations there. I suppose it makes things much easier if you know your son or some other close relative is living on the same landing—there are three landings, are there not? But it is much nicer to live in comfort in London, Mr. Legge— to have a cosy little suite in Bloomsbury, such as you have got; to go where you like without a screw following you—I think 'screw' is a very vulgar word, but it means 'warder,' does it not?"

He walked to the door and turned slowly.

"You won't forget that I expect to meet Mr. Peter Kane and Mr. John Gray tomorrow at my house at half-past ten—you won't forget, will you?"

He closed the door carefully behind him, and, with his great umbrella hooked on to his arm, passed along the corridor into the purview of the astounded Fernando, astounding the jailers on guard at the end.

"Good evening," murmured Mr. Reeder as he passed.

Fernando was too overcome to make a courteous reply.

Stevens saw him as he came into the main corridor, and gasped.

"When did you come in, Mr. Reeder?"

"Nobody has ever seen you come in, but lots of people see you go out," said Reeder good-humouredly. "On the other hand, there are people who are seen coming into this club whom nobody sees go out. Mr. Gray didn't pass this way, or Mr. Kane?"

"No, sir," said Stevens in surprise. "Have they gone?"

Reeder sighed heavily.

"Yes, they've gone," he said. "I hope not for long, but they've certainly gone. Good night, Stevens. By the way, your name isn't Stevens, is it? I seem to remember you"—he screwed up his eyes as though he had difficulty in recalling the memory—"I seem to remember your name wasn't Stevens, let us say, eight years ago."

Stevens flushed.

"It is the name I'm known as now, sir."

"A very good name, too, an excellent name," murmured Mr. Reeder as he stepped into the elevator. "And after all, we must try to live down the past. And I'd be the last to remind you of your—er—misfortune."

When he reached the street, two men who had been standing on the opposite sidewalk crossed to him.

"They've gone," said Mr. Reeder. "They were in that car, as I feared. All stations must be warned, and particularly the town stations just outside of London, to hold up the car. You have its number. You had better watch this place till the morning," he said to one of them.

"Very good, sir."

"I want you especially to follow Emanuel, and keep him under observation until tomorrow morning."

The detective left on duty waited with that philosophical patience which is the greater part of the average detective's equipment, until three o'clock in the morning; and at that hour, when daylight was coming into the sky, Emanuel had not put in an appearance. Stevens went off duty half an hour after Mr. Reeder's departure. At two o'clock the head waiter and three others left, Fernando locking the door. Then, a few minutes before three, the squat figure of Pietro, muffled up in a heavy overcoat, and he too locked the door behind him, disappearing in the direction of Shaftesbury Avenue. At half-past three the detective left a policeman to watch the house, and got on the 'phone to Mr. Reeder, who was staying in town.

"Dear me!" said Mr. Reeder, an even more incongruous sight in pyjamas which were a little too small for him, though happily there were no spectators of his agitation. "Not gone, you say? I will come round."

It was daylight when he arrived. The gate in the yard was opened with a skeleton key (the climb so graphically described by Mr. Reeder was entirely fictitious, and the cut in his trousers was due to catching a jagged nail in one of the packing-cases with which the yard was littered), and he mounted the iron stairway to the third floor.

The window through which he had made his ingress on the previous evening was closed and fastened, but, with the skill of a professional burglar, Mr. Reeder forced back the catch and, opening the window, stepped in.

There was enough daylight to see his whereabouts. Unerringly he made for Emanuel's office. The door had been forced, and there was no need to use the skeleton key.

There was no sign of Emanuel, and Reeder came out to hear the report of the detective, who had made a rapid search of the club.

"All the doors are open except No. 13, sir," he said. "That's bolted on the inside. I've got the lock open."

"Try No. 12," said Reeder. "There are two ways in—one by way of a door, which you'll find behind a curtain in the corner of the room, and the other way through the buffet, which communicates with the buffet in No. 13. Break nothing if you can help it, because I don't want my visit here advertised."

He followed the detective into No. 12, and found that there was no necessity to use the buffet entrance, for the communicating door was unlocked. He stepped into No. 13; it was in complete darkness.

"Humph!" said Mr. Reeder, and sniffed. "One of you go along this wall and find the switch. Be careful you don't step on something."

"What is there?"

"I think you'll find... however, turn on the light."

The detective felt his way along the wall, and presently his finger touched a switch and he turned it down. And then they saw all that Mr. Reeder suspected. Sprawled across the table was a still figure—a horrible sight, for the man who had killed Emanuel Legge had used the poker which, twisted and bloodstained, lay amidst the wreckage of rare glass and once snowy napery.

CHAPTER 28

It was unnecessary to call a doctor to satisfy the police. Emanuel Legge had passed beyond the sphere of his evil activities.

"The poker came from—where?" mused Mr. Reeder, examining the weapon thoughtfully. He glanced down at the little fire-place. The poker and tongs and shovel were intact, and this was of a heavier type than was used in the sitting-rooms.

Deftly he searched the dead man's pockets, and in the waistcoat he found a little card inscribed with a telephone number, "Horsham 98753." Peter's. That had no special significance at the moment, and Reeder put it with the other documents that he had extracted from the dead man's pockets. Later came an inspector to take charge of the case.

"There was some sort of struggle, I imagine," said Mr. Reeder. "The right wrist, I think you'll find, is broken. Legge's revolver was underneath the table. He probably pulled it, and it was struck from his hand. I don't think you'll want me any more, inspector."

He was examining the main corridor when the telephone switchboard at the back of Stevens's little desk gave him an idea. He put through a call to Horsham, and, in spite of the earliness of the hour, was almost immediately answered.

"Who is that?" he asked.

"I'm Mr. Kane's servant," said a husky voice.

"Oh, is it Barney? Is your master at home yet?"

"No, sir. Who is it speaking?"

"It is Mr. Reeder.... Will you tell Miss Kane to come to the telephone?"

"She's not here either. I've been trying to get on to Johnny Gray all night, but his servant says he's out."

"Where is Miss Kane?" asked Reeder quickly.

"I don't know, sir. Somebody came for her in the night in a car, and she went away, leaving the door open. It was the wind slamming it that woke me up."

It was so long before Mr. Reeder answered that Barney thought he had gone away.

"Did nobody call for her during the evening? Did she have any telephone messages?"

"One, sir, about ten o'clock. I think it was her father, from the way she was speaking."

Again a long interval of silence, and then:

"I will come straight down to Horsham," said Mr. Reeder, and from the pleasant and conversational quality of his voice, Barney took comfort; though, if he had known the man better, he would have realised that Mr. Reeder was most ordinary when he was most perturbed.

Mr. Reeder pushed the telephone away from him and stood up.

So they had got Marney. There was no other explanation. The dinner party had been arranged to dispose of the men who could protect her. Where had they been taken?

He went back to the old man's office, which was undergoing a search at the hands of a police officer.

"I particularly want to see immediately any document referring to Mr. Peter Kane," he said, "any road maps which you may find here, and especially letters addressed to Emanuel Legge by his son. You know, of course, that this office was broken into? There should be something in the shape of clues."

The officer shook his head.

"I'm afraid, Mr. Reeder, we won't find much here," he said. "So far, I've only come across old bills and business letters which you might find in any office."

The detective looked round.

"There is no safe?" he asked.

All the timidity and deference in his manner had gone. He was patently a man of affairs.

"Yes, sir, the safe's behind that panelling. I'll get it open this morning. But I shouldn't imagine that Legge would leave anything compromising on the premises. Besides, his son has had charge of the Highlow for years. Previous to that, they had a manager who is now doing time. Before him, if I remember right, that fellow Fenner, who has been in boob for burglary."

"Fenner?" said the other sharply. "I didn't know he ever managed this club."

"He used to, but he had a quarrel with the old man. I've got an idea they were in jug together."

Fenner's was not the type of mentality one would expect to find among the officers of a club, even a club of the standing of the Highlow; but there was this about the Highlow, that it required less intelligence than sympathy with a certain type of client.

Reeder was assisting the officer by taking out the contents of the pigeon-holes, when his hand touched a knob.

"Hallo, what is this?" he said, and turned it.

The whole desk shifted slightly, and, pulling, he revealed the door to the spiral staircase.

"This is very interesting," he said. He ascended as far as the top landing. There was evidently a door here, but every effort he made to force it ended in failure. He came down again, continuing to the basement, and this time he was joined by the inspector in charge of the case.

"Rather hot," said Mr. Reeder as he opened the door. "I should say there is a fire burning here."

It took him some time to discover the light connections, and when he did, he whistled. For, lying by the side of the red-hot stove, he saw a piece of shining metal and recognised it. It was an engraver's plate, and one glance told him that it was the finished plate from which £5 notes could be printed.

The basement was empty, and for a second the mystery of the copper plate baffled him.

"We may not have found the Big Printer, but we've certainly found the Big Engraver," he said. "This plate was engraved somewhere upstairs." He pointed to the shaft. "What is it doing down here? Of course!" He slapped his thigh exultantly. "I never dreamt he was right—but he always is right!"

"Who?" asked the officer.

"An old friend of mine, whose theory was that the plates from which the slush was printed were engraved within easy reach of a furnace, into which, in case of a police visitation, they could be pushed and destroyed. And, of course, the engraving plant is somewhere upstairs. But why they should throw down a perfectly new piece of work, and at a time when the attendant was absent, is beyond me. Unless... Get me an axe; I want to see the room on the roof."

The space was too limited for the full swing of an axe, and it was nearly an hour before at last the door leading to the engraver's room was smashed in. The room was flooded with sunshine, for the skylight had not been covered. Reeder's sharp eyes took in the table with a glance, and then he looked beyond, and took a step backward. Lying by the wall, dishevelled, mud-stained, his white dress-shirt crumpled to a pulp, was Peter Kane, and he was asleep!

They dragged him to a chair, bathed his face with cold water, but even then he took a long time to recover.

"He has been drugged: that's obvious," said Mr. Reeder, and scrutinised the hands of the unconscious man for a sign of blood. But though they were covered with rust and grime, Reeder found not so much as one spot of blood; and the first words that Peter uttered, on recovering consciousness, confirmed the view that he was ignorant of the murder.

"Where is Emanuel?" he asked drowsily. "Have you got him?"

"No; but somebody has got him," said Reeder gently, and the shock of the news brought Peter Kane wide awake.

"Murdered!" he said unbelievingly. "Are you sure? Of course, I'm mad to ask you that." He passed his hand wearily across his forehead. "No, I know nothing about it. I suppose you suspect me, and I don't mind telling you that I was willing to murder him if I could have found him."

Briefly he related what had happened at the dinner.

"I knew that I was doped, but dope works slowly on me, and the only chance I had was to sham dead. Emanuel gave me a thump in the jaw, and that was my excuse for going out. They got me downstairs into the yard and put me into the car first. I slipped out the other side as soon as the nigger went up to get Johnny. There were a lot of old cement sacks lying about, and I threw a couple on to the floor, hoping that in the darkness they would mistake the bundle for me. Then I lay down amongst the packing-cases and waited. I guessed they'd brought down Johnny, but I was powerless to help him. When the car had gone, and Pietro had gone up again, I followed. I suppose the dope was getting busy, and if I'd had any sense, I should have got over the gate. My first thought was that they might have taken my gun away and left it in the room. I tried to open the door, but it was locked."

"Are you sure of that, Peter?"

"Absolutely sure."

"How long after was this?"

"About half an hour. It took me all that time to get up the stairs, because I had to fight the dope all the way. I heard somebody moving about, and slipped into one of the other rooms, and then I heard the window pulled down and locked. I didn't want to go to sleep, for fear they discovered me; but I must have dozed, for when I woke up, it was dark and cold, and I heard no sound at all. I tried the door of thirteen again, but could make no impression on it. So I went to Emanuel's office. I know the place very well: I used to go in there in the old days, before Emanuel went to jail, and I knew all about the spiral staircase to the roof. All along I suspected that the hut they'd put on the roof was the place where the slush was printed. But here I was mistaken, for I had no sooner got into the room than I saw that it was where the engraver worked. There was a plate on the edge of a shaft. I suppose I was still dizzy, because I fumbled at it. It slipped through my hand, and I heard a clang come up from somewhere below."

"How did you get into this room?"

"The door was open," was the surprising reply. "I have an idea that it is one of those doors that can only be opened and closed from the inside. The real door of the room is in the room in Emanuel's office. It is the only way in, and the only way out, both from the basement and the room on the roof. I don't know what happened after that. I must have laid down, for by now the dope was working powerfully. I ought to let Marney know I'm all right. She'll be worried...."

He saw something in the detective's face, something that made his heart sink.

"Marney! Is anything wrong with Marney?" he asked quickly.

"I don't know. She went out last night—or rather, early this morning—and has not been seen since."

Peter listened, stricken dumb by the news. It seemed to Mr. Reeder that he aged ten years in as few minutes.

"Now, Kane, you've got to tell me all you know about Legge," said Reeder kindly. "I haven't any doubt that Jeffrey's taken her to the big printing place. Where is it?"

Peter shook his head.

"I haven't the least idea," he said. "The earlier slush was printed in this building; in fact, it was printed in Room 13. I've known that for a long time. But as the business grew, young Legge had to find another works. Where he has found it is a mystery to me, and to most other people."

"But you must have heard rumours?" persisted Reeder.

Again Peter shook his head.

"Remember that I mix very little with people of my own profession, or my late profession," he said. "Johnny and old Barney are about the only crooks I know, outside of the Legge family. And Stevens, of course—he was in jail ten years ago. I've lost touch with all the others, and my news has come through Barney, though most of Barney's gossip is unreliable."

They reached Barney by telephone, but he was unable to give any information that was of the slightest use. All that he knew was that the printing works were supposed to be somewhere in the west.

"Johnny knows more about it than I do, or than anybody. All the boys agree as to that," said Barney. "They told him a lot in 'boob.'"

Leaving Peter to return home, Mr. Reeder made a call at Johnny's flat. Parker was up. He had been notified earlier in the morning of his master's disappearance, but he had no explanation to offer.

He was preparing to give a list of the clothes that Johnny had been wearing, but Reeder cut him short impatiently.

"Try to think of Mr. Gray as a human being, and not as a tailor's dummy," he said wrathfully. "You realise that he is in very grave danger?"

"I am not at all worried, sir," said the precise Parker. "Mr. Gray was wearing his new sock suspenders—"

For once Mr. Reeder forgot himself.

"You're a damned fool, Parker," he said.

"I hope not, sir," said Parker as he bowed him out.

CHAPTER 29

It was five minutes past two in the morning when Marney, sitting in the drawing-room at the front of the house, heard the sound of an auto stop before the house Going into the hall, she opened the door, and, standing on the step, peered into the darkness

"Is that you, father?" she asked.

There was no reply, and she walked quickly up the garden path to the gate. The car was a closed coupé, and as she looked over the gate, she saw a hand come out and beckon her, and heard a voice whisper:

"Don't make a noise. Come in here; I want to talk to you. I don't want Barney to see me."

Bewildered, she obeyed. Jerking open the door, she jumped into the dark interior, by the side of the man at the wheel.

"What is it?" she asked.

Then, to her amazement, the car began to move toward the main road. It had evidently circled before it had stopped.

"What is the matter, father?" she asked.

And then she heard a low chuckle that made her blood run cold.

"Go into the back and stay there. If you make a row, I'll spoil that complexion of yours, Marney Legge!"

"Jeffrey!" she gasped.

She gripped the inside handle of the door and had half turned it when he caught her with his disengaged hand and flung her into the back of the car.

"I'll kill you if you make me do that again." There was a queer little sob of pain in his voice, and she remembered his wound.

"Where are you taking me?" she asked.

"I'm taking you to your father," was the unexpected reply. "Will you sit quiet? If you try to get away, or attempt to call assistance, I'll drive you at full speed into the first tree I see, and we'll finish the thing together."

From the ferocity of his tone she did not doubt that he would carry his threat into execution. Mile after mile the car sped on, flashing through villages, slowing through the sparsely peopled streets of small towns. It was nearing three o'clock when they came into the street of a town and, looking through the window, she saw a grey façade and knew she was in Oxford.

In ten minutes they were through the city and traversing the main western road. And now, for the first time, Jeffrey Legge became communicative.

"You've never been in 'boob,' have you, angel?" he asked.

She did not answer.

"Never been inside the little bird-house with the other canaries, eh? Well, that's an experience ahead of you. I am going to put you in jail, kid. Peter's never been in jail either, but he nearly had the experience tonight."

"I don't believe you," she said. "My father has not broken the law."

"Not for a long time, at any rate," agreed Jeffrey, dexterously lighting a cigarette with one hand. "But there's a little 'boob' waiting for him all right now."

"A prison?" she said incredulously. "I don't believe you."

"You've said that twice, and you're the only person living that's called me a liar that number of times."

He turned off into a side road, and for a quarter of an hour gave her opportunity for thought.

"It might interest you to know that Johnny is there," he said. "Dear little Johnny! The easiest crook that ever fell—and this time he's got a lifer."

The car began to move down a sharp declivity, and, looking through the rain-spattered wind-screen, she saw a squat, dark building ahead.

"Here we are," he said, as the car stopped.

Looking through the window she saw, with a gasp of astonishment, that he had spoken the truth. They were at the door of a prison. The great, black, iron-studded gates were opening as she looked, and the car passed through under the deep archway and stopped.

"Get down," said Jeff, and she obeyed.

A narrow black door led from the archway, and, following her, he caught her by the arm and pushed her through. She was in a narrow room, the walls of which were covered with stained and discoloured whitewash. A large fire-place, overflowing with ashes, a rickety chair and a faded board screwed to the wall were the only furniture. In the dim light of a carbon lamp she saw the almost indistinguishable words: "His Majesty's Prison, Keytown," and beneath, row after row of closely set regulations. A rough-looking, power-fully-built man had followed her into the room, which was obviously the gate-keeper's lodge.

"Have you got the cell ready?"

"Yes, I have," said the man. "Does she want anything to eat?"

"If she does, she'll want," said Jeff curtly.

He took off his greatcoat and hung it on a nail, and then, with Jeffrey's hand gripping her arm, she was led again into the archway and across a small courtyard, through an iron grille gate and a further door. A solitary light that burnt in a bracket near the door, showed her that she was in a small hall. Around this, at the height of about nine feet from the ground, ran a gallery, which was reached by a flight of iron stairs. There was no need to ask what was the meaning of those two rows of black doors that punctured the wall. They were cells. She was in a prison!

While she was wondering what it all meant, a door near at hand was unlocked, and she was pushed in. The cell was a small one, the floor of worn stone, but a new bedstead had been fitted up in one corner. There was a washstand; and, as she was to discover, the cell communicated with another containing a stone bath and wash-place.

"The condemned cell," explained Jeffrey Legge with relish. "You'll have plenty of ghosts to keep you company tonight, Marney."

In her heart she was panic-stricken, but she showed none of her fear as she faced him.

"A ghost would be much less repulsive to me than you, Jeffrey Legge," she said, and he seemed taken aback by the spirit she displayed.

"You will have both," he said, as he slammed the door on her and locked it.

The cell was illuminated by a feeble light that came through an opaque pane of glass by the side of the door. Presently, when her eyes grew accustomed to the semi-darkness, she was able to take stock of her surroundings. The prison must have been a very old one, for the walls were at one place worn smooth, probably by the back of some condemned unfortunate who had waited day after day for the hour of doom. She shuddered, as her imagination called to her the agony of soul which these four walls had held.

By standing on the bed she could reach a window. That also was of toughened glass, set in small, rusty frames. Some of the panes were missing, but she guessed that the outlook from the window would not be particularly promising, even supposing she could force the window.

The night had been unusually cold and raw for the time of year, and, pulling a blanket from the bed, she wrapped it about her and sat down on the stool, waiting for the light to grow.

And so sitting, her weary eyes closing involuntarily, she heard a stealthy tapping. It came from above, and her heart fluttered at the thought that possibly, in the cell above her, her father was held… or Johnny.

Climbing on to the bed, she rapped with her knuckles on the stone ceiling. Somebody answered. They were tapping a message in Morse, which she could not understand. Presently the tapping ceased. She heard footsteps above. And then, looking by chance at the broken pane of the window, she saw something come slowly downward and out of view. She leapt up, gripping the window pane, and saw a piece of black silk. With difficulty two fingers touched it at last and drew it gently in through the window pane. She pulled it up, and, as she suspected, found a piece of paper tied to the end.

It was a bank-note. Bewildered, she gazed at it until it occurred to her that there might be a message written on the other side. The pencil marks were faint, and she carried the note as near to the light as she could get.

"Who is there? Is it you, Peter? I am up above. Johnny."

She suppressed the cry that rose to her lips. Both Johnny and her father were there. Then Jeffrey had not lied.

How could she answer? She had no pencil. Then she saw that the end of the cotton was weighted by a small piece of pencil, the kind that is found attached to a dance programme. With this unsatisfactory medium she wrote a reply and pushed it through the window, and after a while she saw it drawn up. Johnny was there—and Johnny knew. She felt strangely comforted by his presence, impotent though he was.

For half an hour she waited at the window, but now the daylight had come, and evidently Johnny thought it was too dangerous to make any further communications.

Exhausted, she lay down on the bed, intending to remain awake, but within five minutes she was sleeping heavily. The sound of a key in the lock made her spring to her feet. It was the man she had seen in the early morning; he was carrying a big tray, set with a clumsy cup and saucer, six slices of bread and butter, and an enormous teapot. He put it down on the bed, for want of a table, and without a word went out. She looked at the little platinum watch on her wrist: it was ten o'clock. Half an hour later the man came and took away the tray.

"Where am I?" she asked.

"You're in 'boob,'" he said with quiet amusement. "But it is better than any other 'boob' you've ever been in, young lady. And don't try to ask me questions, because you'll not get a civil answer if you do."

At two o'clock came another meal, a little more tastily served this time. It seemed, from the appearance of the plate, that Jeffrey had sent into Oxford for a new service specially for her benefit. Again she attempted to discover what had happened to her father, but with no more satisfactory result.

The weary day dragged through; every minute seemed an hour, every hour interminable. Darkness had fallen again when the last of the visits was made, and this time it was Jeffrey Legge. At the sight of his face, all her terror turned to wonder. He was ghastly pale, his eyes burnt strangely, and the hand that came up to his lips was trembling as though he were suffering from a fever.

"What do you want?" she asked.

"I want you," he said brokenly. "I want you for the life of my father!"

"What do you mean?" she gasped.

"Peter Kane killed my father last night," he said.

"You're mad," she gasped. "My father is here—you told me."

"I told you a lie. What does it matter what I told you anyway? Peter Kane escaped on the way to Keytown, and he went back to the club and killed my father!"

CHAPTER 31

The girl looked at him, speechless

"It isn't true!" she cried.

"It's not true, isn't it?" Jeffrey almost howled the words. He was mad with hate, with grief, with desire for cruel vengeance. "I'll show you whether it's not true, my lady. You're my wife—do you understand that? If you don't, you're going to."

He flung out of the cell, turning to voice his foul mind, and then the door clanged on her, and he strode out of the hall into the little house that was once the Governor's residence, and which was now the general head-quarters of the Big Printer.

He poured himself out a stiff dose of whisky and drank it undiluted, and the man who had accompanied him watched him curiously.

"Jeff, it looks to me as if it's time to make a get-away. We can't keep these people here very long. The men are scared, too."

"Scared, are they?" sneered Jeffrey Legge. "I guess they'd be more scared if they were in front of a judge and jury."

"That's the kind of scare they're anxious to avoid," said his lieutenant calmly. "Anyway, Jeff, we're getting near the end, and it seems to me that it's the time for all sensible men to find a little home on the other side of the water."

Legge thought for a long time, and when he spoke his voice was more calm.

"Perhaps you're right," he said. "Tell them they can clear tonight."

The other man was taken aback by the answer.

"Tonight?" he said. "Well, I don't know that there's that hurry."

"Tell 'em to clear tonight. They've got all the money they want. I'm shutting this down."

"Who killed your father?"

"Peter Kane," snarled Legge. "I've got the full strength of it. The police are hiding him up, but he did the killing all right. They found him on the premises in the morning."

He sat awhile, staring moodily at the glass in his hand.

"Let them go tonight," he said, "every one of them. I'll tell them myself."

"Do you want me to go?" asked the other.

Legge nodded.

"Yes; I want to be alone. I'm going to fix two people tonight," he said, between his teeth, "and I'm fixing them good."

"Some of the men like Johnny Gray; they were in boob with him," suggested his assistant, but Jeffrey stopped him with an oath.

"That's another reason they can get out," he said, "and they can't know too soon."

He jumped to his feet and strode out of the room, the man following at a distance.

There were two halls to the prison, and it was into the second that he turned. This was brilliantly illuminated. The doors had been removed from most of the cells, and several of them were obviously sleeping-rooms for the half a dozen men who sat about a table playing cards. At only four places were the cell doors intact, for behind these were the delicate printing presses which from morning till night were turning out and numbering French, American and English paper currency. There was not one of the men at the table, or who came to the doors of their cubicles, attracted by the unusual appearance of Legge, who had not served long terms of imprisonment on forgery charges. Jeffrey had recruited them as carefully as a theatrical producer recruits his beauty chorus. They were men without homes, without people, mainly without hope; men inured to the prison system, and who found, in this novel method of living, a delightful variation of the life to which they were most accustomed.

It was believed by the authorities that Keytown Jail was in the hands of a syndicate engaged in experimental work of a highly complicated character, and no obstacle had been placed in the way of laying power cables to the "laboratories." Jeff had found the safest asylum in the land, and one which was more strongly guarded than any he could have built.

His speech was short and to the point.

"Boys, I guess that the time has come when we've got to make the best of our way home. You've all enough money to live comfortably on for the rest of your lives, and I advise you to get out of the country as soon as you can. You have your passports; you know the way; and there's no time like the present."

"Do you mean that we've got to go tonight, Jeff?" asked a voice.

"I mean tonight. I'll have a car run you into London; but you'll have to leave your kit behind, but you can afford that."

"What are you going to do with the factory?"

"That's my business," said Jeff.

The proposal did not find universal favour, but they stood in such awe of the Big Printer that, though they demurred, they obeyed. By ten o'clock that night the prison was empty, except for Jeffrey and his assistant.

"I didn't see Bill Holliss go," said the latter; but Jeffrey Legge was too intent upon his plans to give the matter a moment's thought.

"Maybe you'll see yourself go now, Jenkins," he said. "You can take your two-seater and run anywhere you like."

"Let me stay till the morning," asked the man.

"You'll go tonight. Otherwise, what's the use of sending the other fellows away?"

He closed the big gate upon the car. He was alone with his wife and with the man he hated. He could think calmly now. The madness of rage had passed. He made a search of a little store-room and found what he was looking for. It was a stout rope. With this over his arm, and a storm-lamp in his hand, he went out into the yard and came to a little shed built against the wall. Unlocking the rusty padlock, he pulled the doors apart. The shed was empty; the floor was inches thick with litter, and, going back, he found a broom and swept it clean. With the aid of a ladder he mounted to a beam that ran transversely across the roof, and fastened one end of the rope securely. Coming down, he spent half an hour in making a noose.

He was in the death house. Under his feet was the fatal trap that a pull of the rusty lever would spring. He wanted to make the experiment, but the trap would take a lot of time to pull up. His face was pouring with perspiration when he had finished. The night was close, and a flicker of lightning illuminated for a second the gloomy recesses of the prison yard.

As he entered the hall a low growl of thunder came to him, but the storm in his heart was more violent than any nature could provide.

He tiptoed up the iron stairs to the landing, and came at last to No. 4 and hesitated. His enemy could wait. Creeping down the stairs again, his heart beating thunderously, he stood outside the door of the condemned cell. The key trembled as he inserted it in the lock. No sound broke the stillness as the door opened stealthily, and he slipped into the room.

He waited, holding his breath, not knowing whether she were awake or asleep, and then crept forward to the bed. He saw the outline of a figure.

"Marney," he said huskily, groping for her face.

And then two hands like steel clamps caught him by the throat and flung him backward.

"I want you, Jeffrey Legge," said a voice—the voice of Johnny Gray.

CHAPTER 31

Johnny Gray came to consciousness with a violent headache and a sense of suffocating restriction, which he discovered was due to his wing collar holding tightly in spite of the rough usage that had been his This fact would have been pleasing to Parker, but was intensely discomforting to the wearer, and in a minute he had stripped the offending collar from his throat and had risen unsteadily to his feet

The room in which he was had a familiar appearance. It was a cell, and—

Keytown Jail! He remembered Fenner's warning. So Fenner knew! Keytown Jail, sold by the Government to—Jeffrey Legge! The idea was preposterous; but why not? A timber merchant had bought a jail at Hereford; a firm of caterers had purchased an old prison in the North of England, and were serving afternoon teas in the cells.

Now he understood. Keytown Prison was the head-quarters of the Big Printer. The one place in the world that the police would never dream of searching, particularly if, as he guessed, Jeffrey Legge had offered some specious excuse for his presence and the presence of his company in this isolated part of the world.

The sound of voices came faintly up to him, and he heard a door bang and the clicking of locks; and with that sound he recalled the happenings of the evening. It must be Peter: they had got him too. In spite of his discomfiture, in spite of the awful danger in which he knew he was, he laughed softly to himself.

Above his bed was a window with scarcely a whole pane. But there was no escape that way. A thought struck him, and, leaning down, he tapped a Morse message on the floor. If it was Peter, he could understand. He heard the answering tap which came feebly, and when he signalled again he knew that whoever was in the cell below had no knowledge of the Morse code. He searched his pockets and found a tiny scrap of pencil, but could find no paper, except a bundle of five-pound notes, which his captors had not troubled to remove. Here was both stationery and the means of writing, but how could he communicate with the occupant of the cell below? Presently a plan suggested itself, and he tore off the lapel of his dinner-jacket and unravelled the silk. Tying the pencil to the end to give it weight, he slowly lowered his message, hoping, though it seemed unlikely, that his fellow prisoner would be able to see the paper.

To his joy he felt a tug, and when, a few minutes later, he carefully drew up the message, it was to find, written underneath his own, one which left him white and shaking.

Marney here! He groaned aloud at the thought. It was too light now to risk any further communication. There was a ewer of water and a basin in the cell, and with this he relieved the aching in his head; and when breakfast came, he was ready.

The man who brought in the tray was a stranger to him, as also was the man who stood on guard at the door, revolver in hand.

"What's the great idea?" asked Johnny coolly, sitting on the bed and swinging his legs. "Has Jeff bought a jail to practise in? Wouldn't it have been cheaper to have gone over the Alps?"

"You shut up, Johnny Gray," growled the man. "You'll be sorry for yourself before you're out of here."

"Who isn't?" asked Johnny. "How is Peter?"

"You know damned well Peter has escaped," said the other before he could check himself.

"Escaped!" said the delighted Johnny. "You don't mean that?"

"Never mind what I mean," growled the man, realising he had said too much. "You keep a civil tongue in your head, Gray, and you'll be treated square. If you don't, there are plenty of men on the spot to make Dartmoor a paradise compared with Keytown."

The door slammed in Johnny Gray's face, but he was so absorbed in the news which the man had unwillingly given to him that he had to force himself to eat.

Soon after the man came to take away the tray.

"What's your name, bo', anyway?" said Johnny carelessly. "I hate calling you 'face'—it's low."

"Bill's my name," said the man, "and you needn't call me Bill either. You say 'sir' to me."

"Woof!" said Johnny admiringly. "You're talking like a real screw!"

The door slammed in his face. He had further time to consider his plans. They had taken away his watch and chain, his gold cigarette-case and the small pen-knife he carried, but these losses did not worry him in the slightest. His chief anxiety was to know the exact character of Keytown Prison. And that he determined to learn at the earliest opportunity.

It was late in the afternoon; he guessed it was somewhere in the neighbourhood of four when his lunch came, and he was quite ready to eat it, though a little suspicious of its possible accessories.

"No poison in this, Bill?" he asked pleasantly as he took the bread and cheese from the man's hand.

"There's no need to poison you; we could starve you, couldn't we?" said the other. "If Jeff was here, maybe I'd get a rapping for giving you anything."

"Gone away, has he? Well, prisons are more pleasant when the governor's away. Am I right, Bill? Now what do you say to a couple of hundred of real money?"

"For what?" asked the man, stopping at the door. "If you mean it's for letting you make a get-away, why, you're silly! You're going to stay here till Jeff fixes you."

All the day Johnny had heard, or rather felt, a peculiar whirr of sound coming from some remote quarter of the prison.

"Got electric light here, Bill?" he said conversationally.

"Yes, we have," said the other. "This is a model boob, this is."

"I'll bet it is," said Johnny grimly. "Are you running any electric radiators in my cell tonight, or do you want all the power for the press?"

He saw the man's face twitch.

"Of course, you're running the slush factory here—everybody knows that. Take my advice, Bill—go whilst the going's good. Or the bulls will have you inside the realest boob you've seen."

He had made the guard more than a little uncomfortable, as he saw, and sought to press home the impression he had created.

"Jeffrey's going to shop you sooner or later, because he's a natural born shopper. And he's got the money, Bill, to get away with, and the motorcars and aeroplanes. You haven't got that. You'll have to walk on your own pads. And the bulls will get you half-way over the field."

"Oh, shut up!" said the man uncomfortably, and the conversation ended, as in the morning, with the slamming of the door.

Presently a little spy-hole in the cell door opened.

"What made you think this is a print-shop?" asked Bill's voice.

"I don't think anything about it; I know," said Johnny decisively. "If you like to come to me this evening I'll tell you the name of every worker here, the position of every press, and the length of the lagging you'll get."

The cover of the spy-hole dropped.

Jeffrey was away; that was all to the good. If he remained away for the whole of the night.... He was worried about Marney, and it required all his strength of will not to fret himself into a state of nerves.

In an hour Bill returned, and this time he brought no guard but himself, but, for safety's sake, carried on his conversation through a little grille in the door.

"You're bluffing, Johnny Gray. We've got a fellow here who was in boob with you, and he says you're the biggest bluffer that ever lived. You don't know anything."

"I know almost everything," said Johnny immodestly. "For instance, I know you've got a young lady in the cell below. How's she doing?"

The man was taken aback for a moment.

"Who told you?" he asked suspiciously. "Nobody else has been here, have they?"

"Nobody at all. It is part of my general knowledge. Now listen, Bill. How are you treating that lady? And your life hangs on your answer—don't forget it."

"She's all right," said Bill casually. "They've given her the condemned cell, with a bathroom and all, and a proper bed—not like yours. And you can't scare me, Gray."

"I'll bet I can't," said Johnny. "Bring me some water."

But the water was not forthcoming, and it was dark before the man made his reappearance. Johnny listened at the door; he was coming alone. Johnny pulled up the leg of his trousers and showed those suspenders which were Parker's pride. But they were not ordinary suspenders. Strapped to the inside of the calf was a small holster. The automatic it carried was less than four inches in length, but its little blunt-nosed bullets were man-stoppers of a peculiarly deadly kind.

The door swung open, and Bill stepped in.

"Jeff's back—" he began, and then:

"Step in, and step lively," said Johnny.

His arm had shot out, and the pistol hand of the jailer was pinned to his side.

"This gun may look pretty paltry, but it would blow a square inch out of your heart, and that's enough to seriously inconvenience you for the remainder of your short life."

With a turn of his wrist he wrenched the revolver from the man's grasp.

"Sit over there," he said. "Is anybody in the hall?"

"For God's sake don't let Jeff see you. He'll kill me," pleaded the agitated prisoner.

"I'd hate for him to do that," said Johnny.

He peeped out into the hall: it was empty, and he went back to his prisoner.

"Stand against the wall. I'm going to give you the twice-over."

His hands searched quickly but effectively. The key he was putting in his pocket when he noticed the design of the ward.

"Pass-key, I fancy. Now, don't make a fuss, Bill, because you'll be let out first thing in the morning, and maybe I'll have a good word to say for you at the Oxford Assizes. There's something about you that I like. Give me the simple criminal, and the Lord knows you're simple enough!"

He stepped out of the cell, snapped the lock of the door, and, keeping in the shadow, walked swiftly along the gallery until he came to the open stairway on to the floor below.

The hall was untenanted. Apparently Bill was the only jailer. He had reached the floor when the door at the end of the hall opened and somebody came in. He flattened himself in one of the recessed cell doorways. Two men entered, and one, he guessed, was Jeff. One, two, three, four—the fourth door from the end. That was Marney's door, immediately under his own. He saw Jeffrey stop, heard the too-familiar grind of the lock, and his enemy disappeared, leaving the second man on guard outside.

If Jeffrey had made an attempt to close the door behind him, Johnny would have shot down the guard and taken the consequences. But the man was absent for only a few minutes. When he came out, he was shouting incoherently threats that made the hair rise on Johnny Gray's neck. But they were only threats.

The hall door closed on Jeffrey Legge and Johnny moved swiftly to No. 4. As the door opened, the girl shrank back against the wall.

"Don't touch me!" she cried.

"Marney!"

At the sound of his voice she stood, rooted to the spot. The next second she was laughing and weeping in his arms.

"But, Johnny, how did you get here?… where were you?… you won't leave me?"

He soothed her and quietened her as only Johnny Gray could.

"I'll stay… I think this fellow will come back. If he does, he will wish he hadn't!"

And Jeffrey came. As the grip of strong hands closed on his throat, and the hateful voice of his enemy came to his ears, Johnny's prophecy was justified.

CHAPTER 32

For a second Legge was paralysed with rage and fear. Then, in the wildness of his despair, he kicked at the man, who had slipped from the bed and was holding him. He heard an exclamation, felt for a second the fingers relax; and, slipping like an eel from the grasp, flew to the door and closed it. He stood, breathless and panting, by the doorway, until he heard the sound of steel against the inner keyhole, and in a flash realised that Johnny had secured the pass-key. Quick as lightning, he slipped his own key back into the lock and turned it slightly, so that it could not be pushed out from the other side.

Johnny Gray! How had he got there? He fled up the stairs and hammered on the door of the cell where he thought his prisoner was held safe. A surly voice replied to him.

"You swine!" he howled. "You let him go! You twister! You can stay there and starve, damn you!"

"I didn't let him go. He held me up. Look out, Jeff, he's got a gun."

The news staggered the man. The search of Johnny's clothing had been of a perfunctory nature, but he had thought that it was impossible that any kind of weapon could have been concealed.

"Let me out, guv'nor," pleaded the prisoner. "You've got a key."

There was a third key in his house, Jeffrey remembered. Perhaps this man might be of use to him. He was still weak from his wound, and would need assistance.

"All right, I'll get the key. But if you shopped me—"

"I didn't shop you, I tell you. He held me up—"

Legge went back to his room, found the key, and, taking another stiff dose of whisky, returned and released his man.

"He's got my gun, too," explained Bill. "Where are all the fellows? We'll soon settle with him."

"They've gone," said Jeffrey.

What a fool he had been! If he had had the sense to keep the gang together only for a few hours— But he was safe, unless Johnny found a means of getting through the window.

"In my room you'll find a pistol; it is in the top right-hand corner of my desk," he said quickly. "Take it and get outside Johnny's cell—on the yard side. If he tries to escape that way, shoot. Because, if he escapes, you're going a long journey, my friend."

Inside the cell, a chagrined Johnny Gray sat down on the girl's bed to consider the possibilities of the position.

"My dear, there's going to be serious trouble here, and I don't want you to think otherwise," he said. "I should imagine there were quite a number of men in this prison, in which case, though I shall probably get two or three of them, they'll certainly get me in the end."

She sat by his side, holding his hand, and the pressure of her fingers was eloquent of the faith she had in him.

"Johnny, dear, does it matter very much what happens now? They can't come in, and we can't get out. How long will it take to starve us to death?"

Johnny had already considered that problem.

"About three days," he said, in such a matter-of-fact tone that she laughed. "My only hope, Marney, is that your father, who, as I told you, has escaped, may know more about this place than he has admitted."

"Did you know anything about it?" she asked.

He hesitated.

"Yes, I think I did. I wasn't sure, though I was a fool not to locate it just as soon as Fenner warned me against Keytown Jail. These chaps like to speak in parables, and mystery is as the breath of their nostrils. Besides, I should have been certain that Fenner knew the jail had been taken over from the Government."

He made a careful examination of the bars about the window, but without instruments or tools to force them, he knew that escape that way was impossible. When, in the early hours of the morning, he saw the patient figure of Bill, he realised the extent of the impossibility.

"Good morning, William. I see you're out," he greeted the scowling sentry, who immediately jumped to cover, flourishing his long-barrelled weapon.

"Don't you show your nose, or I'll blow it off," he threatened. "We've got you, Mr. Gray."

"They've got you, alas, my poor William," said Johnny sadly. "The busies will be here at nine o'clock—you don't suppose that I should have let myself come into a trap like this? Of course, I didn't. I squeaked! It was my only chance, William. And *your* only chance is to sneak away at the earliest opportunity, and turn State's evidence. I'm addressing you as a friend."

"You'll never get away from here alive," said the man. "Jeff's going to fix you."

"Indeed?" the prisoner began politely, when a scream made him turn.

"Johnny!"

The shutter which hid the grille in the door was swung back, and the muzzle of Jeffrey's Browning had been pushed through one of the openings. As Johnny dropped flat on the bed, he was stunned by the deafening sound of an explosion. Something hit the wall, ricochetted to the roof, and fell almost at the girl's feet. Before the pistol could be withdrawn, Johnny Gray had fired. A jagged end of iron showed where his bullet struck.

"The time for persiflage," said Johnny cheerfully, "is past. Now you will sit in that corner, young lady, and will not budge without permission." He pointed to the wall nearest the door, which afforded perfect cover, and, dragging up a stool, he seated himself by her side. "Jeffrey's got quite a tough proposition," he said in his conversational tone. "He can't burn the prison, because there's nothing to burn. He can't come in, and he mustn't go out. If he would only for one moment take away that infernal key——"

"There is another door going out from the bath-room," she said suddenly. "I think it leads to an exercise ground. You can just see a little railed-off space through the window."

Johnny went into the bath-room and examined the door. Screwing his head, he could see, through a broken pane, ten square yards of space, where in olden times a condemned prisoner took his exercise, removed from the gaze of his fellows. He tried the key, and, to his delight, it turned. Another minute and he was in the little, paved yard.

Looking round, he saw a high and narrow gateway, which seemed to be the only exit from the courtyard. And on the other side of that gateway was William, the sentry, well-armed and sufficiently terrified to be dangerous. Slipping off his boots, Johnny crept to the gate and listened. The sound of the man's footsteps pacing the flagged walk came to him. Stooping, he squinted through the keyhole, and saw Bill standing, his back toward him, some six yards away. There was no time to be lost. He inserted the key, and the gate was opened before the man could turn to face the levelled revolver.

"Don't shout," whispered Johnny. "You're either discreet or dead. Hand over that gun, you unfortunate man." He moved swiftly toward the terrified criminal, and relieved him of his weapon.

With a gesture, Johnny directed him to the exercise yard.

"Get in and stay," he said, and locked the door, and for the second time, Bill (his other name, Johnny never discovered, was Holliss) was a prisoner.

Skirting the building, he came to the entrance of the hall. The door was open, and with his hand on the uplifted hammer of the gun, and his finger pressing the trigger, Johnny leapt into the building.

"Hands up!" he shouted.

At the words, Jeffrey Legge spun round. There was a boom of sound, something whistled past Gray's face, and he fired twice. But now the man was running, zigzagging to left and right, and Johnny hesitated to fire. He disappeared through the door at the farther end of the hall, shutting it behind him, and Johnny raced after him.

He was in the courtyard now, facing the grille-covered archway. As he came into view, Jeffrey disappeared through the lodge-keeper's door. Johnny tried the grille, but in vain, for a pass-key operates on all locks save the lock of the entrance gate of a prison. That alone is distinct, and may not be opened save by the key that was cut for it.

Covering the lodge-keeper's door with his gun, Johnny waited, and, waiting, heard a rumbling sound. Something was coming down the centre of the archway. The straight line of it came lower and lower. A hanging gate! He had forgotten that most old country prisons were so equipped. Under the cover of this ancient portcullis, Legge could escape, for it masked the entrance of the lodge.

He turned back to the girl.

"Keep out of sight. He's got away," he warned her. "This fellow isn't finished yet."

The gate was down. Jeffrey put on the overcoat he had left in the lodge, slipped his pistol into his pocket and opened the great gates. He had at least a dozen hours' start, he thought, as he stepped into the open....

"Please do not put your hand in your pocket, Mr. Jeffrey," said a plaintive voice. "I should *so* hate to shoot a fellow creature. It would be a deed utterly repugnant to my finest feelings."

Jeffrey raised his hands to their fullest extent, for Mr. Reeder was not alone. Behind him were four armed policemen, a cordon of mounted constabulary, spread in a semicircle, cutting off all avenues of escape. And, most ominous of all, was the deadly scrutiny of Peter Kane, who stood at Reeder's right hand.

CHAPTER 33

For the first time Jeffrey Legge felt the cold contact of handcuffs. He was led back to the porter's lodge, whilst two of the policemen worked at the windlass that raised the hanging gate.

"It's a cop, Craig," he said, for the inspector in charge was that redoubtable thief-catcher. "But I'm going to squeak all I know. Johnny Gray is in this. He's been working my slush for years. You'll find the presses in the second hall, but the other birds have done some quick flying."

"They've all flown into the police station at Oxford," said Craig, "and they're singing their pretty little songs merrily. The Oxford police took a whole carload of them about eleven o'clock last night. Unfortunately, they weren't so ready to squeak as you."

"Johnny Gray's in it, I tell you."

"Oh, how can you say such a thing?" said the shocked Mr. Reeder. "I'm perfectly sure Mr. Gray is quite innocent."

Jeffrey regarded him with a sneer of contempt.

"You're a pretty funny busy.' I suppose Craig brought you here?"

"No," murmured Mr. Reeder, "I brought myself here."

"The only thing I can say about you," said Jeffrey Legge, "is that you're smarter than old Golden—and that's not saying much."

"Not very much," murmured Mr. Reeder.

"But you're not smart enough to know that Johnny Gray has been in this business for years."

"Even while he was in prison?" suggested Mr. Reeder innocently. "The opportunities are rather restricted, don't you think? But don't let us quarrel, Mr. Jeffrey."

The portcullis was raised now, and in a few minutes the girl was in her father's arms.

"Johnny, you've had a narrow squeak," said Craig, as he shook the man's hand, "and there's some talk about you being in this slush business, but I'll not believe it till I get proof."

"Who killed old Legge?" asked Johnny.

The detective shook his head.

"We don't know. But Stevens has disappeared, and Stevens was Fenner's brother. I got it from Mr. Reeder, who seems to have remarkable sources of information."

"Not at all," disclaimed the apologetic Reeder. "I certainly have a remarkable source of information, and to that all credit must go. But I think you will confirm my statement, John, that Stevens is Fenner's brother?"

To Peter's surprise, Johnny nodded.

"Yes, I knew they were brothers; and it is unnecessary to say that their name was neither Stevens nor Fenner. It is pretty well established that the old man gave away Fenner—shopped him for the Berkeley Square job—and possibly Stevens got to know of this, and had been waiting his opportunity to settle accounts with Emanuel. Have you caught him?"

"Not yet," said Craig.

"I hope you won't," said Johnny. "What are you going to do about me, Peter?"

He put his arm round the girl's shoulder, and Peter smiled.

"I suppose I'll have to let her marry you, Johnny, whether you're a crook or honest. I want you to go straight, and I'll make it worth while——"

"That I can promise you." It was Mr. Reeder who spoke. "And may I offer an apology. I'm rather a wolf in sheep's clothing, or a sheep in wolf's clothing. The truth is, my name is Golden."

"Golden!" gasped Craig. "But I thought Golden was out of this business?"

"He is out of it, and yet he is in it," explained Mr. Reeder carefully. "I am an excellent office man," he confessed, in that mincing manner of his, staring owlishly over his glasses, "but a very indifferent seeker of information, and although, when Mr. John Gray Reeder was appointed over me as chief inspector of my department——"

"Here, stop!" said the dazed Craig. "John Gray Reeder? Who is Inspector John Gray Reeder?"

Mr. Golden's hand went out in the direction of the smiling Johnny.

"Johnny! You a busy'!" said the bewildered Peter. "But you went to jail sure enough?"

"I certainly went to jail," said Johnny. "It was the only place I could get any news about the Big Printer, and I found out all I wanted to know. It was a trying two years, but well worth it, though I nearly lost the only thing in the world that made life worth living," he said. "You've got to forgive me, Peter, because I spied on you—a good spy doesn't play favourites. I've been watching you and every one of your pals, and I watched Marney most of all. And now I'm going to watch her for years and years!"

"You see," said Mr. Golden, who seemed most anxious to exculpate himself from any accusation of cleverness, "I was merely the listener-in, if I may use a new-fangled expression, to the information which John broadcasted. I knew all about this marriage, and I was the person who appointed a woman detective to look after her at the Charlton Hotel—but on Johnny's instructions. That is why he was able to prove his alibi, because naturally, that section of the police which knows him, is always ready to prove alibis for other officers of the police who are mistakenly charged with being criminals."

"How did you guess about the prison?"

"Fenner squeaked," said Mr. Golden with a gesture of deprecation. "'Squeak' is not a word I generally like, but it is rather expressive. Yes, Fenner squeaked."

Two happy people drove home together in the car which had brought Marney to Keytown. The country between Oxford and Horsham is the most beautiful in the land. The road passes through great aisles of tall trees, into which a car may be turned and be hidden from the view of those who pass along the road. Johnny slowed the machine at an appropriate spot, and put it toward the thickest part of the wood. And Marney, who sat with folded hands by his side, did not seek any explanation for his eccentricity.